Scribe Publications
GRACE NOTES

Jenny Pattrick is a writer and jeweller who lives in Wellington, New Zealand. She has written fiction and commentary for radio and, with her musician husband, Laughton, songs and musical shows for children.

The Denniston Rose, which was her first novel, has never left New Zealand bestseller lists since it was published in 2003, and has been voted one of the top 100 books in the world by Whitcoulls readers. Jenny Pattrick has since published the sequel, *Heart of Coal*; and a spin-off, *Catching the Current* (all published by Scribe).

GRACE *notes*

JENNY PATTRICK

SCRIBE
Melbourne

Scribe Publications Pty Ltd
PO Box 523
Carlton North, Victoria, Australia, 3054
Email: info@scribepub.com.au

Published in Australia and New Zealand by Scribe 2008

This edition published by arrangement with Random House New Zealand

Cover design by Tamsyn Hutchinson
Printed and bound in Australia by Griffin Press
Only wood grown from sustainable regrowth forests is used in the manufacture of paper found in this book

Pattrick, Jenny, 1936-
Grace notes : a novel

9781921215322 (pbk.)

NZ823.3

www.scribepublications.com.au

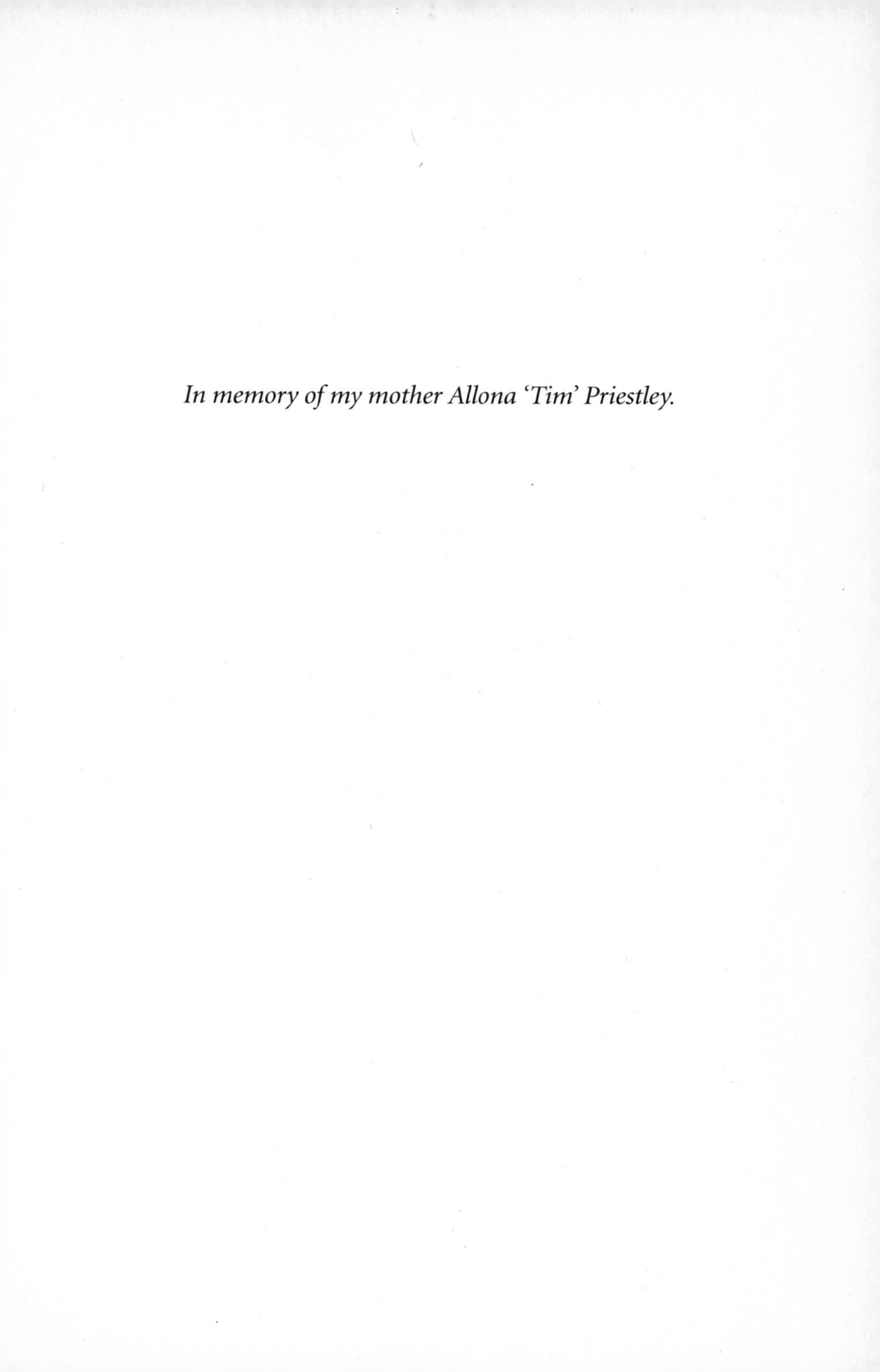

In memory of my mother Allona 'Tim' Priestley.

ACKNOWLEDGEMENTS

Two series, *Grace* and *A Matter for Grace,* broadcast by Radio New Zealand, were the foundation for this novel. My thanks to the staff of Radio New Zealand who, over the years, have encouraged and supported my writing.

I would like to acknowledge the inspirational lives of many friends and relatives whose activities and energies have informed the fictional characters in this novel.

Thanks also to Bill Manhire, who recognised some early spark in the first chapter of this novel and suggested I take it further.

And, as always, I owe a debt to Harriet Allan of Random House New Zealand, whose advice and support I greatly value.

Part One

SECURITY

'Was that Max Friedmann the other day at the outing?' Mildred's words are casual but her eyes watch Grace keenly.

Grace buttons her warm coat with care. The wind is raw today. 'Who?'

'Max Friedmann. That musician who used to live across the park.'

Grace looks across to where Max once lived. The memory is painful. 'Yes,' she says, 'I believe it was.'

'You and he seemed very chatty.' Mildred has never cared much for Max Friedmann. A loud, overexuberant man, given to waving his hands about.

'No, no,' says Grace, smiling, 'chatty is definitely not the word. He's as deaf as a post. I hadn't seen him in years — it would have been rude not to say hello.'

Mildred is about to add further warnings about speaking to any Tom, Dick and Harry who might approach, even if they had been neighbours in the past, when her attention is caught by shrieking children, bouncing among the branches of the trees along the park.

'You should do something about those children,' she says 'They're ruining your trees.'

Grace laughs. 'They're people, not garden pests, Mildred.' She climbs into Mildred's car and, with a twinge, reaches for the seat belt. 'And anyway,' she adds, 'they are my security system.'

Mildred doesn't follow up this interesting lead. At the

moment, driving the car takes serious attention. Both women buckle in — a frustrating and sometimes competitive activity — and set their eyes firmly on the road ahead. At a sedate pace, the little car climbs the hill, ventures into the main road and, this corner having been conquered with some success, runs along, quite jaunty, down to the Community Centre.

Each winter, on the first and third Thursday, Mildred takes Grace to bowls. Second and fourth they go in Grace's car. Sherry afterwards, in the passenger's house, is a reward for having exercised.

Les Comfrey is laying down the last mat when they arrive. Four green parallel stripes divide the wooden floor, and four sets of balls — six black, six brown — wait ready for the first game. Almost all the players are ready to begin. Grace is pleased: like everyone here she enjoys punctuality. She leaves her apricot slice in the kitchen. Afternoon tea is a serious function of bowls day.

Grace discovers that she is to play with old Mrs Peddie. This is a mixed blessing. Old Mrs Peddie is ninety-three. Her mind wanders, she is nearly blind and very deaf, but somehow she still manages to put down a mean bowl. When playing with old Mrs Peddie you can be pretty sure to win your game. On the other hand Grace, who is a younger and much more erratic player, will have to put up with Mrs Peddie's loud advice on technique.

The games begin. Grace's balls do not behave as she intends them to.

'Oh dear, oh dear, Emily,' roars old Mrs Peddie, who had a brush with hearing aids twenty years ago and found them wanting. 'Oh dear, dear me. I think, Emily, that you must have the wrong bias. Do think before you put the ball down.'

Old Mrs Peddie's memory for names has gone completely, so the criticisms, though broadcast throughout the hall, are not damaging in a personal way.

Then it is Mrs Peddie's turn. Grace places a brown ball in her papery hand. The old lady holds it close to her face and inspects it slowly. Searching for what? Grace wonders. Another couple of minutes are spent getting the bias sorted out. Shakily, old Mrs Peddie lowers herself and sends the ball on its way. She shades her eyes and peers up the mat, but the distance is too far.

'Let's see how the balls lie,' she shouts, 'before we plan the next move.'

Grace sighs. She can see very well that her partner's ball is snugly tucked into the jack.

'You do need tolerance when it comes to the aged,' says Les, who is eighty. It always takes two people to move old Mrs Peddie. With Grace supporting one arm and Les the other she moves in on the jack with the deliberation of an advancing tank. Bending low over the collection of balls, she peers and mutters till she is satisfied, then the trio retreat heavily down the mat to prepare for the next ball. Games with old Mrs Peddie tend to be lengthy and physically exhausting.

'Good exercise, though,' says Mildred at afternoon tea. 'You'll have walked twice as far as me.' Mildred has enjoyed a nice sociable game. 'Cynthia and I both played terribly,' she says, 'and neither cared a fig!'

The discussion over the cakes is satisfying. Several pieces of interesting information are relayed. The big house on Pembroke Road has gone for four hundred thousand. At least three bowls members went to the auction and can verify the price. There is general discussion over what this figure reveals about property values in the area. Grace recognises the group's comfortable glow — she feels it herself. They are all making modest capital gains.

'Was that Max Friedmann at the outing, Grace?' says Les. 'He made a beeline for you, I noticed. Never even glanced in my direction.' He winks.

Grace sighs. Les's innuendoes are as subtle as a sledgehammer. 'His hearing is bad, Les,' she says, 'He simply said hello and moved on. I haven't seen him in years.' She shifts the conversation quickly on to burglaries.

There have been none in the neighbourhood this week, it seems. This is unusual. Les puts it down to the weather.

'Let's face it, your burglar is just your average man in the street,' he says. 'They don't like working in the rain any more than the rest of us.'

'Oh, I don't accept that, Les,' says Grace, who loves an argument. 'A burglar is not average, no, no — a burglar is someone sick, out of step, not average at all.'

'You may say that, Grace, but I've had experience: I've been at the coalface. Your burglar today is just Mr Average with knobs on. No different under the skin from any of us.'

No one is going to accept this. Les Comfrey tends to get carried away, that is accepted, but you have to draw the line. Several severely aberrant burglaries are remembered and re-examined. Shirley Chan's nephew was knocked down by someone on the run — 'almost certainly a burglar'. Les is reminded of the time he wrote to the paper on the subject of burglar mentality — '. . . you weren't talking about Mr Average then, Les.'

Les clears his throat, straightens his already immaculate tie. 'Well, well, there may be something in what you say, but I still maintain . . .' His voice trails away. Concessions do not come easily to him.

The next topic is the funeral. A former member of the bowls club has died and Cynthia, the young Mrs Peddie, aged seventy-one, organises cars and food for Friday. Mildred and Grace offer to combine forces on something a bit out of the usual in the savoury line. Grace enjoys the funerals. You have to expect them, at their age, and the occasions are usually warm supportive affairs, serving a real purpose.

Finally Mildred herself reveals that the post office, empty for the last ten months, is going to open as a French bakery. Dawn, the hairdresser, has told her. Dawn is an excellent source of gossip, and Mildred's hair appointment that morning has been nicely strategic. This bit of news is a coup. A French bakery! It is an exotic and stylish idea with some appeal. However the consensus is that the neighbourhood is too conservative.

'I'm not keen on French bread,' proclaims old Mrs Peddie. 'The crusts are difficult.'

'There'll be a short honeymoon,' predicts Les Comfrey, 'and then it'll go under. French pastries! What a pie in the sky!' Les has been in retail.

'They'll be serving pies too, yes,' agrees Mildred. Grace notices the slip but no one comments. They all mishear from time to time.

Grace's little back room is warm, the curtains pulled. The heater has been left on two — a safe level — and the tray with decanter and glasses waits on the coffee table. Mildred notices that Grace has shifted her Drawbridge print; the new position jars slightly, as does the altered arrangement of the seating. Grace *will* move her things around — you never know where you are. Mildred has not changed one piece of furniture since her husband died fifteen years ago. But she holds her peace. The sherry ritual is one of the highlights of the winter week, and nothing will be allowed to mar it.

Over the next couple of hours they will drink two glasses of medium sweet sherry, fully justified in terms of sociability and exercise. Their free-flowing conversation will canvass books, politics, gardening, new recipes and the neighbourhood. The friends are good conversationalists. They face each other squarely in strong light so that the sight of the words can aid their sound.

'Now what's all this about the children being your security system?' says Mildred, sipping her sherry neatly and with pleasure.

The security theory is an excuse, Grace knows, but she argues it with vigour, nevertheless. Forty years ago, when she and Reg married and bought the big old bungalow next to the park, they planted a row of trees all down the fence.

'One day,' Reg said, 'our grandchildren will climb these trees.'

There were no grandchildren. Reg died, and then Gillian, Grace's only daughter, committed suicide. Family hopes and expectations died with her.

These days, though, the schoolchildren use the trees for forts and wild shrieking games. Their heads poke out from piney branches; they bounce and swing and call to one another from tree to tree like bright tropical birds. Interval and lunchtime, on five sunny days a week they give shape to Grace's day and she loves them. She knows branches get broken, that some trees are becoming misshapen. So she makes rational arguments to justify the chattering flocks.

'Look, Mildred, at who they are,' she says, ready to make her case. 'You have, in my trees, a cross-section of all the homes in the neighbourhood. Now if all those children know and like me, take stories home about the nice old lady in number forty-four, their bigger brothers, if they have a tendency towards being the rough element, are going to respect my home. Don't you think?'

Mildred looks most doubtful. 'No, no, Grace, you're surely optimistic. Your cross-section of the neighbourhood are probably spying in your windows to see what they or their big brothers might plunder!'

'Well, I may be optimistic. Yes. I prefer to be. Those cheerful boys and girls are *good* people.' Grace omits to say that she sometimes goes out with a plate of biscuits or sweets. She suspects Mildred would frown on it; like feeding a cat that wasn't yours.

'I *believe* in human nature, Mildred,' she says.

'Well, don't we all — so do I — but we must be sensible at our age, Grace. Human nature comes in all shapes.'

'Yes, but if we fear the worst, we encourage it to happen. No, Mildred, I put my trust in those children.'

'At least get deadlocks, Grace. You're a sitting target, next to the park here.'

Mildred has deadlocks, bolts on all windows, a random lighting system for when she is away and a burglar alarm connected to the police station.

But Grace smiles and pours a second glass each.

'There's a word I can't get in the *Listener* crossword,' she says.

A month or two later, a child falls from a tree on the park and breaks a leg. It is not one of Grace's trees but a larger one on the other side. The headmaster places all trees out of bounds. Grace cares more than she likes to admit. Now that the branches have lost their multicoloured blooms her trees have altered. They lean in on her; they are darker. She is aware of their bulk.

At about this time too, Grace receives an emergency summons from Mildred. Returning home from a visit to her Auckland daughter, Mildred has discovered a burglary. The thieves, negotiating all traps and alarms, have removed several pieces of heirloom jewellery.

'Nothing's damaged, that's a blessing,' says Mildred. But still they feel an alien presence vibrating in Mildred's immaculate living-room. Two stiff brandies are helping with the shock.

'But Mildred, how did they get in? What about your alarm?'

'Well, you see, they cut a neat hole in my bathroom window. The police, who have been most kind, recommend a deadlock between bathroom and hall. I'm looking into it.'

'Oh but what a rigmarole, going to the toilet at night!'

'Well, that's true, Grace, yes I hadn't thought of that. Perhaps my locksmith will have some advice.'

They both laugh, thinking of the delicacy of this discussion.

'I must say, Mildred, that you're taking it all very well. I would be angry to lose my family pieces.'

'To be honest, I never cared much for that old stuff. And it's insured. At least they waited till I was away before they broke in. I'm grateful for that.' Grace realises that Mildred is rather enjoying the drama. The bowls club will certainly hear all the details.

Back home Grace wonders why her rambling old 'sitting target' has been spared, while Mildred's neat fortress was singled out. She has deadlocks fitted on front and back doors — mainly as a gesture of solidarity. It is a mistake: the balance has shifted. Mildred, having survived attack, becomes a confident expert on the subject, while Grace stands in the dark hall, behind her new deadlocks feeling trapped.

Uneasy thoughts and fears come and go at will. Her beloved bookshelves lining walls in every room now seem to loom. The sunny spare room proclaims its yawning void. Memories of her daughter's death return.

'This is ridiculous,' she says out loud, after a depressing week of these dark thoughts. 'At my age I should be in control.'

First she phones the locksmith and outlines her request. Then the headmaster. That gentleman clears his throat nervously at the sound of her voice and Grace smiles. It is not the first time she has crossed swords with him. Recently it was the use of the apostrophe on the billboard announcing the school fair. Grace makes an appointment for later in the day.

Promptly at 3.15 she steps out over the park, coat firmly buttoned, red woollen hat snug over her short grey hair. Grace is a small woman, not much taller than the children who are heading home. One child waves to her. Grace is ridiculously pleased.

In the headmaster's tiny office Grace removes hat and gloves, accepts a cup of tea, then comes briskly to the point. 'I have come about the children in the trees.'

Mr Gregory is clearly relieved. 'Ah well, we're ahead of you this time, Mrs Brockie. You'll be pleased to know that we have a new school policy: No climbing in the trees on the park during playtime or lunchtime. If the children return to the park after they have reached home, that's another matter. Out of our hands. It is a public park after all.'

Grace raises an admonishing finger. 'I am well aware of your new policy and I am *not* pleased with it.'

'Your reason?'

Mr Gregory's voice has an edge of condescension which Grace notices. He thinks she is going gaga. She glances quickly at the points she has noted down. 'Climbing trees is surely a healthy activity,' she says, her words a little too loud in her own ears. 'I have always believed that it fosters nimble limbs and an adventurous spirit. Today's youth are far too prone to slump in front of the television set. You yourself, Mr Gregory, have been a sportsman of some achievement' (she smiles at him here, hoping the flattery will bear fruit) 'and I know you approve of plentiful activity in the school curriculum.'

Mr Gregory's patient smile remains. 'You're perhaps not aware that one of our pupils suffered a serious injury falling from those trees. It would be a dereliction of duty . . .'

Grace interrupts. It is time for her trump card. 'That child fell from a tree by the tennis courts — a mature pohutukawa, a tree whose limbs are notoriously difficult to climb. The trees over on my side of the park, on the other hand, are *Cupressocyparis leylandii*, ideal for the purpose. They're also lower to the ground. There has never, to my knowledge, been an accident from these trees.'

Mr Gregory scribbles on his notepad. Grace thinks her arguments may be swaying him. He frowns though and looks across at her squarely. 'Mrs Brockie, the child's mind is a simple one which needs simple rules. A blanket policy will be obeyed; a complicated one will not.'

Grace breathes in sharply. She cannot let this man get away with such a blatantly inaccurate statement. 'The child's mind, Mr Gregory, is vastly more complex than the adult's. Surely you, as a senior educator, know this. The child's mind is capable of learning new languages, and new skills at a frightening speed. Our older brains are set. They simply do not compare. Tell the children they may climb on the trees along my fence but not the tennis court ones and they'll understand in a trice. It is a grave mistake to underestimate the power of a child's mind.'

Owen Gregory's smile widens. He spreads his hands. 'Well, there's no sign *your* brain has set, Mrs Brockie. I'm puzzled by your attitude, though. Surely the children are noisy? Are ruining the trees?'

Grace smiles gently and lines up her parting shot. 'My dead husband and I planted those trees. We wished our children and grandchildren to play in them. As you may not be aware I have no family.' She lets a pause develop, concentrates on pulling on her gloves. 'I would be grateful if you could see what you can do,' she says with what she hopes is a wistful smile.

Next week over Thursday sherry, Grace feels her old sharp self again.

'I know you won't approve, Mildred,' she says, 'but I've had my deadlocks removed.'

'Oh Grace, surely you're being foolhardy?'

'Well, it's worth it to me, Mildred, I feel ten years younger. And the children will be back in the branches from tomorrow. The headmaster took a little persuading, but my arguments won in the end. Cheers.'

Mildred pauses, her eyes lively. 'Well, if those deadlocks are going begging, Grace, perhaps you could spare one for my bathroom door. Cheers.'

Grace raises her glass. The two women sip together, and laugh till the tears run.

July 13th 1993

Grace Brockie!
I was thinking about you only an hour before, and there you suddenly were with birds flying about your head. A vision in a bird sanctuary! I gathered you were with a group of superannuitants? Most of them looking much older than you I might say! The years have treated you well. Of course I was dying to settle down for a good chat but my hearing is not up to conversing in a group — and you were busy with your friends anyway. Was that Mildred Catherwood with you? She has aged.

But then it is, after all, twenty years since we moved up here. We rather lost touch, I'm afraid, with friends at church and round the park. I meet Les Comfrey from time to time and he says you have stayed on in the big house. Good for you! It must be difficult, though, without a man to do the heavy work.

You have perhaps not heard that Ilona passed away last year. It was cancer in the end, though she had been unwell for some time. You and she were good friends in those days so I thought you would like to know. It has not been easy for me since. I am not very house-trained I'm afraid, though I had learned a few basic dishes during Ilona's illness. However, no sense in moping I always say! Hence this letter. I have decided to plan a luncheon, once a month, and invite five or six people. I will make myself cook a new dish each time. And always include new faces too. It is Hinemoa's idea. She is a good positive soul — my district nurse. Now, what about coming? This would be for Monday 26th of this month at 12.30 pm. Les says you still drive. It will take you an hour and a half, but we are not short of time at our end of life, are we? Don't be daunted by the Rimutakas. The road over the hill is well graded now and you will sail over!

If this seems presumptuous, please forgive me. I greatly admired you during your troubled times — your husband's death, and then Gillian's tragedy. I still can't bear to think of that wasted life . . . that brilliant talent! How strong you were! Surely we have things in common now to share and enjoy. Do come.

Yours faithfully,
Max Friedmann

Friday July 16th 1993

Dear Max,
How pleasant to hear from you so soon after our meeting, and thank you for your kind invitation to lunch. Unfortunately, I do not drive on the open road any more. I feel my sight and my reactions are not up to fast driving, and know how irritating a slow driver on the highway can be.

I'm so sorry to hear that Ilona died. No, I hadn't heard. Some watch the papers for that kind of thing but I find it morbid.

You may be interested to know that I'm teaching a little music appreciation class for the University of the Third Age. Have you heard of this organisation? It is purely voluntary and is run for, and by, retired people. An old ex-teacher like me — or anyone else with a skill — shares it with whoever's interested. I'm sure there is a branch up your way. They may be glad of your services. Certainly much of what I teach I learned at your house concerts. Do you still play?

I am sorry to decline your invitation. Enclosed is my recipe for tuna fish pie. It is very simple to make but tastes special. You may find it useful.

Yours faithfully,
Grace Brockie

Tuesday July 27th

Dear Grace,
Thank you for the recipe. You are right, it is delicious. I used it for the Monday luncheon and it was highly praised. Ilona had a good herb garden which I have kept up so I added a little chopped garlic-chive and parsley. I hope you don't disapprove. Nothing venture, nothing learn! To be honest, my tastebuds have lost their edge — it takes a good curry to make an impression — but my ladies enjoyed it.

You mention the University of the Third Age. What a coincidence! Indeed there is one in the Wairarapa, and I am chairman of it! There are many classes out here and my responsibility is the organising. I'm afraid I don't teach or play music now. My deafness is quite severe and going to a concert or listening to music irritates me beyond belief. All I hear are the bass notes. If I know the piece really well I can supply the upper register from memory, but it is not the same, as you can imagine.

But enough of that. Try to look on the bright side as Hinemoa my district nurse says. She is young — late forties I'd say — but full of wisdom. You'd like her I'm sure.

Now Grace, I feel you are being unadventurous. If the open road daunts you, take the train to Carterton and I will meet you at the station. It does us all good to have a change of scenery. Any day will do — it doesn't have to be a Monday. And if a group is not what you enjoy, we could have a lunch for two and you can pass judgement on tuna fish pie à la Max. You were pleased to see me at the bird sanctuary, don't pretend otherwise! Take hold of life while it's still here to enjoy!

I enclose a little pin which belonged to Ilona. I'm sure she would like you to have it. I do not have a daughter and Martin's wife doesn't seem to be interested.

Yours,
Max

P.S. Most Wednesdays I work for the Alliance Party, but any other day suits. M

Sunday 1st August 1993

Dear Max,
The little pin is exquisite and your thought is kind, but I feel I cannot accept. Perhaps you don't realise what a treasure it is. Surely you have granddaughters who are interested or who will become so. Fashions change. A piece like this should stay in the family.

I must admit, though, that I wore it to Chamber Music last night — New Zealand String Quartet playing Bartok very well indeed — and my friend remarked how well it went with my winter suit. Do you realise the stones are real? I will keep it till someone is coming out your way . . . Les Comfrey perhaps. You were certainly reckless, Max, to send it by ordinary mail. But the thought was kind and I appreciate it. Ilona was a good friend when I needed one.

It is surprising to hear you have joined the Alliance. I always took you for someone rational. I'm sending you a copy of the Labour manifesto. They have made their mistakes but I am convinced they are still the only viable choice.

I think not about the train trip. I am not naturally timid, but I have always found the Wellington Railway Station a little frightening. Perhaps we should stick to the odd letter. It is an undervalued art-form these days.

Thank you again for the pin. I will keep it safe, meanwhile.

Yours faithfully,
Grace

Tues 3rd August 1993

Dear Max,
I realise you couldn't hear a word I said when you rang just now, so am writing down what I said. My friend is a woman, my neighbour, Mildred, whom you surely remember. We share a Chamber Music ticket. I am definitely not involved in any intimate relationship. Nor do I want to be, Max. I could not bear to go through another separation.

Yours faithfully,
Grace

P.S. Which hearing aids do you use? I have switched to Philips in both ears and find them excellent. I am sending you a brochure.

Sunday 8th August 1993

Dear Grace,
Sorry, I made a fool of myself, ringing you like that. Why do I try? I know I can't hear. I use hospital hearing aids — don't know what sort, but I can't afford the fancy ones. Never mind — I'm deaf as a post anyway, and have my own ways of coping.

Now. Why didn't I think of it before? Les Comfrey is the answer to our problem! He comes out here often on a Sunday to visit his son. I saw him today and he says he'll be happy to bring you out, drop you at my place and take you back again. What could be better? Please don't find another excuse: friendship is all I'm suggesting. We need to enjoy life and I can't stand my children feeling they've got to entertain me. Their entertainment is to plonk themselves in front of TV and watch sport anyway. Wouldn't it do you good to get away from home and the sad memories of the park now and then?

You may laugh at the Alliance and I'll admit some of them are a bit wet behind the ears — especially the Greens. Their ideas are right, but the endless soppy guitar songs! Thank goodness I can't hear them. Watching them is quite bad enough. But they are idealists, Grace, and I feel we badly need a bit of that . . .

Well, to be honest, a friend dragged me along and I enjoy the company. You may be right. Come out and convince me!

Les says he could bring you out next Sunday — 15th — after church. I go to the Quakers' meetings now and then. At least I don't feel I'm missing anything! But I'll be home in time to cook lunch (I have something new in mind). If the weather is fine we could drive down to the lake.

Les Comfrey is a friendly soul and will be good company for you on the car trip, but he's not the right person for you, Grace. Your mind has always been so open and lively! His is rather a closed book, don't you think? I will think up some issues to challenge you on and we can have a bit of good rational argument when you get to my place.

Please keep the brooch.

Yours,
Max

TANGI

'There is no way,' says Les Comfrey, 'that you're going to get me to a tangi.'

'I agree with Les. Why don't they have a proper funeral?' Mildred looks flushed, not at all her usual cheerful self.

'But Mildred, they were bowls members for years. Marge has asked us specially. What would it look like if we refused?' It is Cynthia's responsibility to arrange trips to funerals and she takes the job seriously.

'Cynthia's right,' says Grace. 'We have to go. Marge used to organise funerals for us herself, didn't she? No, Mildred, we'll just have to screw up our courage.'

'It's not a matter of courage. Not at all.' Les is flushed now too. 'It's a matter of principle. All that mumbo-jumbo. We're Christians. We go to Christian funerals.'

'For heaven's sake, Les, a tangi is Christian!'

'Well, it's not to me, Grace. You're always up with new ideas…'

'New! Christian tangis must have been happening for a hundred and fifty years. More!'

'You're not going to persuade me, Grace. We brought religion here. And we brought churches. A church is a proper place for a funeral, that's flat. Now I've nothing against Marge and Bob. Salt of the earth, both of them. Bury Bob in a Christian church and I'd be there like a shot. But you won't catch me at a tangi.'

There is a silence after this speech. Afternoon tea at the

bowls club is usually good-natured.

'My son says you didn't pick up your Sunday paper this week, Grace,' says Shirley Chan. 'Have you been ill?'

'Oho! Not ill.' Les is keen too, to change the subject. 'She's got a new boyfriend in the Wairarapa.'

'Don't talk nonsense, Les.' It is Grace's turn to flush. 'I just visited Max Friedmann. An old friend.'

'Max Friedmann?' says Mildred. 'You didn't tell me about this, Grace.'

'Didn't I?'

'I would've come too. You have to be careful with Max.'

'Well,' says Les, 'I know what I'm saying on this one, and I'd say there's more to it than old friends. Eh Grace?'

'She's blushing!' shouts old Mrs Peddie. 'Tell me why. I missed it!'

'Oh you lot!' Grace is used to this teasing — it'll be someone else next week. 'You'd turn a handshake into a deep romance. Now come on. I know this tangi is upsetting for some of us but we can't just hide from it.'

'Tangi?' Old Mrs Peddie pronounces it correctly, to everyone's surprise. 'Are you Maori, Grace? What tribe?'

It takes a while to get old Mrs Peddie onto the right track.

'Of course we have to go,' she shouts. 'We'll all be treated like royalty, being our age. And no shirking, Les, you're our senior man.'

'I'm not so sure about that,' says Jack Chan. 'How old are you, Les?'

'Eighty.'

'Well, I'm eighty-three. That makes me the elder of the group, surely.'

'But I'm your senior in the *bowls* club, Jack. You only came last year.'

'I thought you weren't coming to the tangi, Les?'

'I'm not. I've had my final word on that. It's the principle of the matter we're discussing here. I'm the senior male in this club.'

'Then you must come,' says Cynthia Peddie. She is very definite. Grace likes this practical woman, who is the youngest in the club. 'Mother is right,' says Cynthia. 'When they see all these white heads coming onto the marae, they'll make us very welcome. They're used to people who don't know what to do.'

'I don't like feeling a fool,' says Mildred. She is looking most agitated, almost tearful.

'We'll stick together, Mildred,' says Grace to her friend. 'It'll be new to me too.'

'It's all very well for you, Grace — you like change and new things. I like the old ways.'

'You won't find it difficult, my dear,' shouts old Mrs Peddie. 'I've been on lots of marae. My son is a Maori.'

'Rubbish, Mother,' says Cynthia. 'It's my son, not yours, and he's *married* to a Maori. You have Maori great-grandchildren.'

'Whatever. What's the difference? We are Ngati Porou.' Old Mrs Peddie faces the group aggressively. 'What tribe were Bob and Marge?'

'Mother, we have enough problems without bringing in tribal rivalry. Now, Marge asked us and she'll be counting on some cooking. Les, will you bring your sausage rolls as usual?'

'I told you . . . '

'Les, you're our elder. They'll expect you to give a little speech about Bob — on our behalf. English will be quite acceptable.'

'A speech, eh?' Les takes out his diary. 'Well, I am free. How long should I speak for do you think?'

'Quite briefly,' says Cynthia quickly.

'No that's not right, Cynthia, you know it's not,' says Mrs Peddie, 'Some of the speeches go on for ever. Just feel free, Les . . . '

'In English, the speech should be brief.' Cynthia eyes her mother-in-law sternly. A wasted effort; old Mrs Peddie's senses do not pick up subtleties.

'Oh well, I suppose I'll have to put aside principles if it's expected,' says Les, 'Yes, Cynthia, I'll do sausage rolls.'

'Your principles will have more to cope with when we die, Les,' says Shirley Chan. 'We're Buddhist. I'll do a pav, Cynthia.'

'I never knew that, Shirley!' says Grace. 'How interesting. I have great respect for some of the Buddhist teachings. We must discuss them together some time.'

Shirley looks at her husband in alarm.

'My advice is,' booms old Mrs Peddie, 'wear shoes you can take off without bending down, take a warm coat, and ask one of the old people where the loos are as soon as you get there. I love going on the marae.'

'Oh Mother, you've only been once.'

'I'm afraid I won't be coming,' says Mildred. 'I can't manage it. I'll send a cake, Cynthia.' The speech is formal but everyone notices the trembling chin. There is a pause. As usual it is Grace who breaks the silence.

'I was in the French bakery yesterday,' she says, 'talking to Jean-Pierre. He says his mother has just come out to join him. She hardly speaks any English and is lonely, so I suggested she come along to bowls.'

'Oh Grace,' says Les Comfrey, 'give us a break!'

Sunday 17th October 1993

Dear Max,
Thank you for the splendid day last week. I must admit that I look forward greatly to our fortnightly arrangement. You are quite right; we have much in common. Especially the love of a good argument!

I'll enclose this note with your book. It was kind of you to lend it to me but I'm afraid I just can't get up enthusiasm for science fiction. There are so many *good* books to be read. That Orycx creature was completely unbelievable. Grotesque. If you want to describe human emotions and human dilemmas, why not put them into a human body? I did a lot of skipping I'm afraid.

Have you read Maurice Gee? I have just finished his latest — *Going West* — and it is excellent. Now *there* is something worth reading! I will bring it next time I come out. You should read his *Plumb* trilogy. You would relate to the deafness!

By the way, Max, do you think we could try a different arrangement for my next visit? Perhaps I will brave the railway station after all. That gives us more flexibility. To be honest, Les cannot resist teasing at bowls. It's all quite harmless but I think it upsets Mildred. She is less broad-minded than me and cannot quite approve, I think, of our relationship.

I did enjoy our walk on the beach last Sunday. Palliser Bay is so wild! Those mountains of driftwood — like careful sculptures formed by some giant artist! I thought of Paul Klee for some reason. Why, I wonder?

You are quite right, it does me good to get out of this house from time to time. Much though I love it. I know you suggest that it is too large and labour-intensive for a single woman, but I have found my way of dealing with that — keep one or two rooms warm and let the unwanted ones rest behind closed doors. At any rate how could I leave my garden? It's full of colour these days and my cherry tree a riot of blossom. I could watch the wax-eyes feeding in it all day.

I read an interesting article in *Time* last week about ozone. Are you aware that ozone has twice as much oxygen as ordinary air? No wonder we felt exhilarated on the beach.

I hope you are taking frequent doses of ozone yourself, Max. You have a nasty hack and are perhaps not aware how loud it sounds to others. Have you had it seen to? It is all very well to say you don't believe in doctors, but there comes a time when good sense overrides principles. Your cough has reached that time.

Would Tuesday week (October 26th) suit you for a visit? I will park near the station and pick up the car on the way back. I could catch the early train (7.58 am) and return by the 3.15 pm. I don't enjoy driving at night. May I bring something special for our lunch this time?

With kind regards,
Grace

P.S. I know you suggested Mildred might like to come out too sometime, but I think we'll leave that for the present. Mildred's daughter is visiting on Tuesday week. She will be too busy to notice my absence.

Tuesday 19th October 1993

Dear Grace,
Tuesday it is! I will be waiting at the station never fear. The 7.58 sometimes comes in a little early so I will drive down in good time.

Perhaps I will accept your offer of a lunch dish. I must admit I felt a little downhearted after my last effort. You were very kind, but perhaps I should stick to the recipe book. I tell you what — I'll branch out and make a cake for afters. That will test me.

Now Grace. About science fiction. You are simply missing the point about the genre. You mustn't judge it on the same terms as a novel. Science fiction is about imagination and moral dilemmas. Style and character development are secondary. Anyway I thought Orycx was an enormously interesting character. You mustn't be put off by a few orifices in the wrong place. Orycx's attitude to social structure was fascinating, I thought. No, I will argue against you on this one. It does us good to puzzle about the future — where the human race is going. I will try you on another book. Perhaps I started you on something too technical.

You ask whether I have read Maurice Gee? Grace, do you realise that he writes science fiction? Aha . . . I have caught you out this time!

I'm beginning to have reservations about the Alliance. They all mumble into their beards and I can't follow a word of what they say. A naïveté shines like a halo over everything they do. Ideals are important in their place of course, but where is the rigour, Grace?

Perhaps the Nats are a safer bet after all.

Now what is all this about Paul Klee? I have been back to my *Visual Dictionary of Art* and am still completely in the dark about your connection. Grace, Klee's work is one-dimensional, linear, almost childlike. I can find no reference to sculpture. How can you possibly relate his work to those piles of driftwood, which I agree are magnificent? Are you perhaps confusing Klee with LeBrun or Le Corbusier? (obviously I became fascinated, in my book, by the L's!). Or even Picasso — with some reservations. Give me your arguments for Klee at once!

Oh, I'm loving all this! You are a wonderful woman, Grace and I have completely fallen in love with you. I look forward to your visits enormously and I know you're happy out here too, so don't pretend you aren't!

I have a plan which I will put to you when you come out, but start thinking about it now: I know you need time to look at all facets of a proposition. It would be unwise, as you have pointed out several times, to make major shifts at our age, but how about spending two or three days with me, say once a fortnight? I could come in and do the same with you in the alternate weeks. We could do things together — go to exhibitions and films.

Now I know you will be reluctant at first, but just let the idea simmer until next Tuesday. I promise to marshal powerful arguments. We could have such fun!

I look forward to seeing you next Tuesday.

With love,
Max

P.S. Would I be rushing you to suggest you stayed overnight on Tuesday? The 10.15 am is much less crowded for the trip back. M

Monday 1st November 1993

My dear Max,

Thank you so much for the most enjoyable day, Tuesday last.

I travelled home safely and the system with the car worked perfectly. The 3.15, by the way, was not crowded at all — almost empty in fact.

I hope you found that my mushroom quiche did you for another day. For my part, I've had a slice of your zucchini and carob cake each day with my lunch. It has lasted well. A most adventurous start! I would suggest that if you try it again, and I think you should, you use baking soda instead of baking powder. One level teaspoon. I think that will do the trick. The flavour is interesting, though; you are very inventive!

I'm just putting my feet up after a visit to the public library. Usually we go to Karori but this week Mildred and I decided to tackle the trip to town. The choice is much better, and Mildred says the books are cleaner there. She may be right. It's the first time I have been inside the new building and I must say I was shocked. The shelves are metal! So is the furniture. You know me well enough, Max, to know I'm not averse to new ideas, but it seems so wrong to put a wonderful warm thing like a book in a shelf made of white metal mesh. You *must* have wood for a bookshelf. The whole atmosphere is wrong. Mildred agreed. We nearly turned round and walked out again.

However we persevered and got out an interesting collection. Well, Mildred's taste is not mine. Historical romances are her cup of tea. I took out a Maurice Gee science fiction from the young adults. I don't hold out much hope. I note he wrote them some time ago; he has no doubt matured since then.

I realise that with all the argument during my visit last week, we never revisited poor old Paul Klee. I fear you are being too literal, Max. Of course the piles of driftwood aren't visually similar to Klee's work, but *in spirit*, don't you think? The whimsy, the random placement of this and that. I could imagine a giant Klee tossing logs around and having fun with what happened. I must say that when I looked up LeBrun and Le Corbusier in the dictionary, I could see no likeness at all to our airy beach sculptures. Both illustrations show lumpy, cloddish work which I find depressing. You will need to find a more imaginative artist if you are to persuade me away from Klee. I think you just took down the dictionary and it fell open at L!

Now, about your plan, Max. I promised to think it over and I certainly have been doing just that. You are very persuasive and kind. You are right, I do enjoy our times together, but I don't feel I'm ready to commit to a regular arrangement. We should be wary, I feel, of becoming too dependent on each other.

And have you thought of your son's feelings? What would Martin feel if he arrived and found me ensconced?

However, I do have a suggestion to make. What

about your coming in to me in a fortnight's time (Tuesday 16th) and staying overnight? There is a very well-reviewed film on at the Penthouse, in Spanish, with subtitles. I always enjoy subtitles — much easier to follow the plot. And for you, of course, it would be ideal. We will be in good company: I've noticed that the hearing-aid brigade turn out in force when there are subtitles! There's a pleasant restaurant in Brooklyn and we could have dinner there first. I would like you to be my guest.

Mildred will be down south, visiting her Christchurch daughter so I will be quite free. I think, if this arrangement suits you, we will keep it to ourselves. Mildred might find it difficult to cope with.

Max, you have brought pleasure into my life. I hope my caution over the visits does not hurt you.

Yours,
Grace

P.S. You may not bring your wretched politics with you!

Sunday 7th November 1993

My dear,
What did I tell you! What a triumph for the Alliance! I was at Martin and Sheila's last night — both true blue, wouldn't you know — and by the end of the evening they could scarcely bear to talk to me. Next election we will have twenty seats in Parliament. That'll shake things up a bit.

About Tuesday week — of course you haven't hurt me. I'm overjoyed at your invitation! I know I tend to rush things and will keep on dripping away at the stone, never fear!

What a splendid idea to go to the Spanish film. We never have subtitles out here. And the restaurant sounds a real treat. But only if I pay my share. I know you are a woman of means, my dear, but I can afford the odd fling. We must start as we intend to go on.

I will bring in a zucchini and carob Mark II for you — with baking soda, don't worry!

My son thinks I'm coming in to see the ear specialist and staying in town with a friend. He assumes the friend is Hamish!

You, my dear Grace, are the best possible specialist for me. I always hear you. We understand each other, that's why.

However I must take you to task over the bookshelves. Have you any idea what wooden shelves cost these days? If metal ones keep down the rates let's have them, I say. I believe all materials have their charm. There is a solid dignity about good steel that is worthy of any book.

Now, how about my staying over for the Wednesday night too, and then I can make up my own mind about the library? If Mildred is away who is there to be offended? We could take a picnic lunch onto the wharf if it is fine. I read about Para Matchitt's controversial new bridge sculpture and I want to see for myself.

But only if you are happy about that, Grace. I must be patient.

I certainly will not leave my politics behind. They are the spice of life! Especially now.

Bless you my dear,
your loving Max

Monday December 6th

My dear Max,
Perhaps we should postpone any more overnight visits till things settle down a bit. Your stay with me worked so easily, and I just assumed staying with you would be the same. I'm not used, you see, to remembering about family. Martin is your son after all and I'm sure he has many fine qualities.

I do hope, my dear, that you have not been too hurt by the incident. And how is your health? I am most anxious but know ringing will get me nowhere. Perhaps you could phone me and give a bulletin? I will not try to talk; I know how frustrating that is to you.

You are probably rather in the dark over the whole business. Martin and his wife do not try to include you in conversation, and I noticed that several times they deliberately lowered their voices. I find that utterly inexcusable.

To be fair, I expect it was rather a shock for them to find me there. But I couldn't leave you all night with a high temperature — you needed nursing. And I was perfectly respectable in your pyjamas and old dressing gown.

Martin and that wife of his came in at the back door while I was preparing your breakfast. They were all dressed up. On their way to church they said. They looked down their noses at me, there's no other word for it — stood in the doorway in complete silence, like censorious teachers waiting for an explanation from a badly behaved pupil. I wish I had taken the time to get dressed properly. But I was anxious about you, Max. Martin said something under his breath to his wife about 'Dad's new girlfriend'.

Then the wife — Sheila, is it? — screwed up her mouth as if she'd tasted something nasty, and proceeded to give me a lecture on how their religion didn't approve of what I was doing; that marriage was sacred; that 'Dad's' place was with his family; and that they could look after you perfectly well themselves.

The fundamentalists have a lot to answer for. I cannot bear that sort of narrow-minded bigotry. It gives Christianity a bad name. But I was upset to be found standing there in your pyjamas, and didn't feel I could argue. Or that it was my place to.

I'm sorry, my dear. Have I made it difficult for you with your own family?

Martin seemed embarrassed by the whole thing. By me. It should be laughable but at the time I was not able to face him. Clearly he wanted to tidy me away and out of sight as quickly as possible. He said that Sheila would stay and look after you and suggested that he ran me to the station. It's very demoralising to be treated like that. They made me feel like some naughty child caught with her hand in the cake tin. I know you would have liked me to stay, Max, but I felt out of place. I could not stop my tears.

Did you understand why I left? I have a feeling that perhaps you didn't. Your hearing aids were out I noticed.

Perhaps we have been unwise to let our friendship develop this far.

Do, please, let me know how you are.

With love,
Grace

P.S. What a curse intolerance is!

Thursday Dec 9th 1993

Dear Grace,
Thank you, thank you for your explanation. I was completely in the dark. In fact I wondered whether my kiss, that night, had offended you.

Now you must absolutely disregard anything Martin and Sheila say. They are not bad people, just limited, and I've told Martin so in no uncertain terms!

Why, if they care so much about my well-being, weren't they nursing me themselves, I said! I pointed out that I'm a perfectly rational adult with a right to make my own friendships; that they should be happy that I'm enjoying life, which is more than they seem to do in their colourless little world. Then I threw in a few home truths about the dangers of their narrow brand of Christianity.

My health is improving.

I have put down my foot about your visits. How arrogant our children are, to think that they know what's best for us! But Grace, what's the use in ranting on? I doubt if I will ever open their minds. Their religion blinkers them. Or is it some other fear? I've made it clear to them that our friendship will not alter my will.

However they have been quite kind these last few days, bringing in meals. I must try to be understanding, I suppose.

Sometimes I fear for the world. What makes this fundamentalism so popular? *Your* daughter would not have embraced it, I'm sure. If she had lived. Now there was a free spirit! And a talented one. My best pupil by far. We must talk about Gillian sometime, Grace, you mustn't shut it out.

I'm a bit down today. Please come. I'm not up to travelling in to you yet. We mustn't let the limitations of other people destroy our friendship. It is wholesome and good.

Your loving
Max

P.S. Did you vote for MMP in the end? I did of course but am having a few qualms about the future. Already MPs are jumping boat and talking about new parties. A bunch of chameleons worried about their pay packets. Consensus and coalition make sense in theory; if only politicians had the intelligence and maturity of you and me! Now we would make a coalition of some style, my dear, and have the country back on track in no time. M

Sunday Dec 12th, 1993

Dear Grace,
Why don't you write? You mustn't let Martin and Sheila's attitude influence you. They will get used to things. They are middle-aged adults, with their own lives. I will not let them push me into some stifling mould of their own making. My wishes are more important than theirs, Grace, when it comes to us.

Or have I upset you myself? Please let me know. Curse my ears, that I can't ring you up and find out!

With warm regards,
Max

Tuesday Dec 14th 1993

Dear Grace,
Was it what I said about Gillian? I can't believe that you would let Martin and Sheila keep us apart. If you don't want to talk about Gillian, we won't.

Grace, Grace, what is happening?

Yours,
Max

P.S. I've just had a terrible thought. Did my smoked eel and pickled walnut pâté give you food poisoning? Perhaps I had left it out of the fridge too long. I know I'm sometimes forgetful over fish. M

Thursday Dec 16th 1993

Dear Mildred,
Do you remember me? Max Friedmann from over the other side of the park? Perhaps Grace has told you about our friendship.

I am worried about Grace — have not heard from her all week. Could you check she's all right? It's not like her to leave mail unanswered.

I do not hear well on the phone, but if you could be bothered to drop me a line, I would be most grateful.

Yours sincerely,
Max Friedmann

P.S. It occurs to me that your postman may be at fault. You may wish to check on him — or her. Cutting corners — literally! — is not uncommon these days.

Saturday 18th December 1993

My dear Max,
You old bear, you are panicking for no reason at all! I am perfectly all right and suffered no ill effects from your pâté. It was one of your more successful efforts, I thought.

Mildred has been very ill and I've been tied up, keeping her company. Do you realise that it's only ten days since that incident with Sheila and Martin? I have put that all behind me, Max. As you say, we are independent adults and can choose for ourselves.

But being caught in your pyjamas severely undermined my confidence. I am not as emancipated as I thought!

Please do not worry Mildred further about us. She has problems enough of her own. Last Tuesday she suffered a mild heart attack but didn't call the doctor for two days. I thought it was just a bit of flu — she stayed in bed, and I took the odd casserole over (my tuna fish pie, actually). Then she became very low and I insisted that she rang the doctor. He has diagnosed the heart attack and pneumonia. Poor Mildred. She's been packed off to hospital, which she detests. Her Auckland and Christchurch daughters have come and are staying in the house.

So now I have time to write to you, you impatient man. The daughters are visiting Mildred all the time and I feel it is their right to have her undivided attention. Besides I get lost in the public hospital's parking system. Last time I went there my car disappeared completely. I spent half an hour walking round searching for it. I'm so small I can't see over the car roofs to get an overview. Finally a nice tall attendant helped me. Even he had trouble. I was in completely the wrong place — totally disoriented! They should take more care with signs. It could have been an emergency.

Well now, Max, I trust you are recovered. There seems to be too much illness in my life at present. Judging by the flow of letters you must have some energy at least! Have you been to the doctor about your chest? Mildred's reluctance was not a good idea, and you should learn from it.

Why are you so anxious, Max, for me to talk about Gillian's death? It was painful enough at the time. Do I seem bitter or guilt-ridden to you? It was, after all, twenty years ago. I had thought I had come to terms with that terrible night. But if it seems important to you, write to me about it. It is too tender a subject for a shouted conversation.

Dear Max, I would love to come and visit you. If you're not up to the driving, I can catch a taxi from the station. What about Tuesday week — the 28th? I could stay overnight and return on the Wednesday afternoon. Shall we call that our Christmas? You will want to spend the real thing with your family. I'll bring some good nourishing pea and ham soup and a pudding I make which is crammed with Vitamin C.

You need building up.

Affectionately,
Grace

Monday 20th December 1993

My dearest Grace,
Damn and blast! Everything seems to be conspiring to frustrate us. Adam has just written to say he has leave and will come up to spend Christmas with me. Our children just assume that we have nothing better to do than sit and wait anxiously for their next visit. It didn't occur to Adam to ask whether the timing suited me. But I suppose he means well.

Would you like to come out just for the day? Or perhaps we should wait till he goes back. You know how difficult three-way conversations are for me. I'm longing to see you again though, my dear Grace.

What a relief to get your letter today and hear that all is well. Please give Mildred my best wishes. Persuade her if you can to leave the hospital. She will only die in there. Looking out over the park from her own bed would be a better cure.

For some reason I can't stop thinking about Gillian, and the night of her death. You are so like her, Grace — same lively eyes, same perky way of moving, same burning intelligence. Getting to know you again has brought back all those memories. She had so much talent, Grace! There's no doubt that she could have become an international soloist. Well, you know that. She and her violin sang a magic that was irresistible. It was a privilege to teach her. How could she waste her life like that? The first piece she played, that night — it was our last house concert, we could never face another — was quite outstanding. Do you remember it? A Bach piece, very simple, but utterly right. That strength should have been enough to anchor her. Why wasn't it?

She came back, later that night, to apologise. Not for her tantrum, or the rude things she said to the audience — that didn't worry her — but for messing up the trio. I don't think I ever told you that, did I? She was rather drunk and I'm afraid I was disapproving. Tried to lecture her about professionalism. I wanted to go over her mistake with her, point out where she came unstuck.

I didn't even recognise she was in trouble or that she may have been looking to me for help. I was too tied up with the music you see, Grace. Ilona would have seen the need; would have done something wise, but she was asleep by then.

Gillian just walked away without a word. In the middle of my gabble. I shudder to remember it. Max Friedmann, the celebrated violinist, lecturing earnestly about stress and dynamic, blind to his best pupil's despair. I could have saved her.

Well, my dear, I can hear what you are thinking: it is Max, not Grace, who needs to talk about Gillian. True. If I had behaved with more care that night you might now have a daughter and grandchildren to share your Christmas.

I cannot even make music for you myself any more.

Oh dear, this is getting maudlin. Forgive me.

My broad beans are wonderful this year — a bumper crop. Do you like them? And the fruit trees have set well, despite my neglect of them lately. When Adam goes and you come out, you shall have a full tour of the garden.

I am slower at getting things done, which is annoying. However the cough is improving — without any fancy drugs from the doctor. Hinemoa came yesterday to drain my ears. They have become infected. She's just like you, harping on about drugs, hospital etc. Don't worry, I'm a tough old boot.

Take care, my dear. Please write quickly. I could not bear to hurt you.

Your loving
Max

P.S. Happy Christmas! A bottle of champagne is hidden from the family, waiting for you! M

Christmas Day 1993

Dear Max,
Happy Christmas to you too! I'm just back from dinner with the Peddies. It was kind of them to invite me, but I found it a noisy affair — I am not used to small children screaming underfoot. In the end it was old Mrs Peddie who saw my discomfort and rescued me. What a surprising woman she is — far deafer than me, extremely unstable on her pins and almost blind, and yet she somehow sensed that I couldn't cope well with the endless senseless questions little ones throw at you. That old lady suddenly clapped her hands and bellowed for the whole rampaging house to hear — 'Little ones! Story time! Gather here!' And miraculously they did. A good dozen of them, all skin colours, sitting quiet on the floor round her chair.

'Can we have a story out of your head?' one little great-grandchild asked. 'Naturally,' said old Mrs Peddie, 'what else can I tell with these old eyes?' And away she went, the most high-flown adventures involving every one of the children on magic quests and hidden treasure and I don't know what else. Most of the adults spellbound too. You have to admire the old lady: most days she is maddeningly off the play — away with the fairies and ready for the nursing home — and then she comes out with an impromptu story that I would have to write out and redraft and then read from the paper to even approach her skill.

Well, for all that, I'm happy to be in my quiet home again. I am writing to you sitting in the garden at my little table. The sun is setting and the hills beyond the harbour have taken on that wonderful deep purple you noticed last time you were here.

Don't worry about Adam coming — it's only a few weeks, and you'll enjoy seeing him. Family is important. You must never turn from your boys. We can wait till after Adam's visit. Perhaps by then you will be up to a trip in to see me.

Meantime these letters may lay Gillian's ghost to rest. You are right — it is you who needs to talk about her, Max. Do you realise she was rather in love with you? Not just as a star-struck pupil loves her maestro but in a personal way. She loved your energy and zest, and your uncompromising commitment to music. I used to be jealous of you! It was always Max this and Max that . . . But now it adds richness to our relationship, discovering for myself the qualities that Gillian saw.

There's no point in blaming yourself for her death. We all failed her in one way or another. Yes, I knew she had gone back to see you that night. Ilona told me. She knew I needed to hear everything. Perhaps you might have saved her but I doubt it, Max. Gillian had been mildly suicidal for some time. She also had a serious drinking problem. She was more than 'rather drunk' that night; she was awash with alcohol. The post mortem showed that. I always thought you knew about her drinking. Ilona did — but maybe she didn't talk to you about it? Gillian was clever at concealing her alcoholism. Perhaps your lessons were the only moments she kept sober for. But in the last few weeks she was always drunk, I think.

Was it Reg's death, I wonder, that started her off? They were wonderfully close, in a way that I just couldn't understand — such totally different people. Or perhaps it was the pressure of university and the concerto competition. Whatever it was, Max, I was no help to her, either. I discovered her drunk in her bedroom once, months before her death and we had a flaming argument. She stormed out, climbed a tree in the park and sat in the branches there while I pleaded below. She just sat, waxen-pale, with tears rolling down her cheeks. Not a sound. In the end I went away. She threw herself off the branch — or fell — and broke a leg. She said she was trying to kill herself.

Psychiatric help might have saved her then, but I didn't force the issue. It was easier to believe she would grow out of the problem, and that her music would win in the end. I know I failed her, Max, but she also failed herself. And you. It helps to think that way — or it helps me anyway.

I tell you what, Max: you have been right about me after all. It has done me some good to take out Gillian's death and look at it again. I've been sitting here for a good fifteen minutes looking out towards the viaduct, and the view somehow seems less harsh — just a view. It is good to talk about it with someone who loved Gillie too. Thank you.

This morning I took flowers and a little gift across

for Mildred's daughters to take to her. They tell me she's sinking. They have sent for her son who lives in Malaysia. Mildred is not speaking, they say. I'll go to the hospital in the morning, but dread it. It's not easy to talk to her with the daughters standing round. I will miss her dreadfully.

Do you know, Max, I find it strangely unsettling to think that I now live in a National electorate. Where are they all? Everyone at bowls voted Labour or Alliance. Although now I think about it, some of our less outspoken members didn't voice their views. I feel I have failed, and will try harder next election. I hope to have you back in the fold before then. We shall have much to argue over!

Make sure you take Vitamin C night and morning. Kiwifruit and tamarillos are very rich sources. Better than oranges and less acid.

All the best, my dear,
Grace

P.S. You gave much pleasure to Gillian — think about that.

Sunday Jan 2nd 1994

Dear Grace,
This place has been a madhouse for the last week. Be pleased you decided not to come. Adam has rushed from one project to another. I trail round trying to help but generally getting in the way.

First he reroofed the shed. Then the driveway needed patching. Yesterday he replaced some rotten weatherboards and today he's painting the kitchen.

Now he's insisting that I need a cleaning lady. He wishes to pay for her, as a gift to me! What nonsense. If I can't see the dirt, it doesn't bother me. You never complained about a dirty bath or toilet. Nor does Hinemoa. Adam is just finickity. Have you noticed lawyers are often like that? He whips my underclothes away and into the wash before I've had a chance to wear them in. Electricity bills obviously mean nothing to him. He has also bought me a new kettle which switches itself off and has rewired my perfectly good old iron. He means well, I suppose, but you can't deny it's insulting. I've told him so and it makes no difference.

I will divert him tomorrow by asking him to look at the car. Now it really does need attention and should take him the next week to fix.

Thank you for speaking so openly about Gillian. She was the daughter I always wished I had. You and Ilona talked it all out at the time, but I could never bear to.

When she stormed out of the concert, that night, where did she go? Do you know? And did she really try to kill herself or was she just so drunk she fell? If you can bear to tell me what you believe happened, Grace, I would be grateful.

No, I hadn't realised she was either suicidal or alcoholic. I'm not very sensitive about those things, I fear. I was completely absorbed in teaching her, and in her wonderful potential.

I see the Brodsky Quartet will be playing the Shostakovich cycle at the festival. Now, Grace, you are to go and remember every detail to tell me. Those string quartets are my absolute favourites. Take someone with you — you can afford a double ticket. I don't like to think of you in town on your own at night.

Adam leaves next Saturday. Why don't you come out on Sunday for a day or two and see me, all clean and tidy in my polished house? I'm driving again and getting about. Or will be when Adam has dealt with the car. We might take a picnic down to the river.

Oh my Grace, you are so dear to me!
Max

P.S. You might as well give up hope of converting me. I am veering towards National. We need stability, Grace! Coalitions are a disaster.

Wednesday 5th January 1994

Dear Max,
I smiled at the thought of Adam sprucing up your house! You should accept his offer of a housekeeper. I have to say, Max, that I did notice the state of your bathroom and toilet, and sometimes cleaned it if you weren't watching! Hinemoa did the same. You are absent-minded about cleanliness. Adam is a good boy and cares about you. Even if he is a lawyer!

Sunday won't suit me, I'm afraid, for coming out. But the following Tuesday (11th) would be ideal. I'm looking forward so much to seeing you again.

Mildred has rallied! She seemed to be on her last breath. I visited her in hospital four days ago and just sat for a while, chatting about whatever came into my head. It was hard to keep going with Mildred looking so ill. Her son had arrived from Malaysia, and everyone had paid their last respects. I thought I was saying goodbye to her.

And then next morning she turned a corner, her breathing improved and she took some food. Perhaps my silly chatter did some good. Her daughters say she will probably be discharged next Sunday and be nursed from home. I would like to be here to welcome her.

Her children are a bit thrown. They mill round the house at a loose end. They have all dropped their jobs and travelled to her death-bed, and now it seems she'll be fine in a week or two! She's a good battler just like you. I'm so pleased.

There is nothing more to know about Gilly's death, Max. It was sad. And pointless — that's all.

She was already drunk when she arrived to play at your house concert. The Bach was easy to manage and she played so well because the drink released her emotions. She recognised that, I think. She felt she needed the alcohol to 'free' her music but then she could not stop.

During the supper break, I imagine she got into your liquor. She was over the edge for the trio and tripped up on the first difficult passage. Her fury with the audience and you and the cellist were simply a cover-up for her own despair.

I followed her out and walked back with her over the park. I've often relived the next hour. Said different things. Listened harder to what she was really saying.

She was very depressed. She felt that her career was ruined; that you would drop her; that she would never be able to control her drinking. She spoke quite a bit about you, Max. How she only lived for your good opinion, and how she had ruined everything. I couldn't help feeling a bit put out that her obsession with music and with you was unhealthy. She hardly seemed aware that I existed. So perhaps I was less sympathetic than I might have been. But I did see that the drink and depression were serious. I determined to get her to a specialist next day.

She went quiet when we got home. I assumed she would sleep off the drink and feel more rational in the morning. I went to bed, and was woken later by the police.

You know the rest, Max. She slipped away and came to see you. You mustn't blame yourself. The problem was hers. I would like to believe that she was so disoriented she simply lost her balance, but the coroner was probably correct. She jumped. In a way, though, I feel it *was* an accident. You are right in seeing her music as an anchor. But the drink, her talent and her temperament were an unlucky combination that night. I believe her jump was a defiant fling, rather than a serious attempt at suicide.

That is how I see it, Max. Her death emptied us both for a while. Now, perhaps, we are joined by having shared her life.

I look forward greatly to seeing the new, spic-and-span Max on Tuesday 11th. I am relieved that Adam is repairing your car. If only he could persuade his dad to drive more slowly and not to argue while behind the wheel!

With love,
Grace

Friday 7th January 1994

Dear Mrs Brockie,
I am not sure whether the family have let you know that Max Friedmann sadly passed away yesterday. His health had been failing for some time. I expect he told you he had lung cancer.

But it was a sudden heart attack in his sleep that carried him off.

I am enclosing your letter which arrived today. It is unopened. I am not sure whether you would want Martin and Sheila to read it, so I took the liberty of removing it quietly when it came in the mail.

I am so sorry if this news is a sudden shock to you. You and Max seemed to have such fun together. You were very good for him, he talked often about your visits.

The funeral is on Monday, 11 am, at Martin and Sheila's church.

Max died quite peacefully. I came this morning and laid him out. He looked lovely.

Kua mahue koe me to pouri. Tangi tonu, tangi tonu. You are left with your sadness. Let your tears fall.

Arohanui,
Hinemoa Spark, District Nurse

Monday 10th January 1994

Dear Mr and Mrs Martin Friedmann, and Mr Adam Friedmann,
Please accept my condolences on the death of your father. Max was a good friend to me over many years. I will miss him as I am sure you will also.

Enclosed is a diamond and pearl brooch which Max gave to me last year. I do not believe he understood its value. Such a piece should remain in the family, and I always intended returning it.

Yours sincerely,
Grace Brockie

TRYING HARDER

'She's made up her mind to go,' says Dr Ramachandran. 'There's nothing more I can do.'

The words are like a physical blow to Grace. Pink spots appear on her cheeks. She looks up sharply at the doctor.

'Surely that's not possible. Mildred is not an Aborigine. We are not in some African village. How can you say such a thing?'

'Well, it may sound strange to you, Mrs Brockie, but I assure you it's quite common. I've tried, and failed, to change her resolve.'

Grace frowns and looks away across the park. This morning the trees are shining, but her spirits are not lifted by the sight. The doctor waits politely, his hand still on Mildred's wrought-iron gate. Grace turns back to him.

'Dr Ramachandran, we simply do not behave like that here. I don't mean to offend, but . . . '

'But you do, Mrs Brockie,' says the doctor gently. 'You do. I have been practising in New Zealand for twenty years. Your friend has no clinical illness. She has recovered well from the pneumonia. But she has decided not to live any more.'

'You don't just decide things like that.'

'Not often, it's true. But in Mrs Catherwood's case that is exactly what has happened. Her children were informed she was dying. They all came to pay their last respects. They farewelled her. Then she recovered. She now feels rather foolish, as if she has outlived her welcome. So she has decided to die.'

Grace presses her lips together and looks at the doctor squarely. He leans down smiling, but when he puts a kind hand on her shoulder, she moves away sharply.

'We'll see about that,' she says and leaves Dr Ramachandran smiling in the sun.

Some of the bowls group gather at Cynthia Peddie's place to discuss the crisis.

'Can it be true, Grace?' asks Cynthia. 'Surely they can do something?'

For once, Grace is at a loss.

'I simply don't know,' she says and sighs. 'Mildred just lies in bed, won't eat — or can't. I can't rouse her interest in anything.'

Grace doesn't say out loud what she really feels. She is irritated with Mildred. Why should Mildred decide to die when she, Grace, her good friend, is still alive? Does their friendship mean nothing to her?

'In this country,' says Les Comfrey, 'people do not decide to die. Mildred must get a second opinion. Dr Ramachandran has missed something.'

'But Les,' says Cynthia, 'we all go to Dr Rama. We know how good he is.'

'No, Cynthia, we must face facts. Mildred will have some named illness with a proper cure. We don't go in for pagan mumbo-jumbo here. Now my brother has a good doctor with a solid New Zealand training. Perhaps Mildred should see him.'

'I tend to agree with you, Les,' says Grace.

Everyone looks startled at this. Grace and Les traditionally take opposite views, particularly where racial bigotry is involved. Grace does not elaborate, but lowers her head, feeling trapped.

'Aren't we forgetting,' says Shirley Chan, 'that this is Mildred's choice. She doesn't want another opinion. She's happy with Dr Ramachandran. To me it's quite understandable that she should want to die at her own convenience. Her children have said goodbye. She feels this is an appropriate time.'

'But surely . . . ' Grace cannot hold back the outburst. 'Surely she must value my friendship . . . and all of you at bowls,' she adds, just in time.

'Well yes,' says Shirley, smiling in her calm way, 'but family is so much more important. It is family we come back to in the end.'

'Why? Why do you say that?' Grace knows she is speaking too loudly, but her outrage needs a voice. 'All Mildred's children and grandchildren live somewhere else. Mildred and I do things together almost every day. Or did. I can't believe that some slight embarrassment with family farewells could be more important to her. She must be ill.'

'She has no right,' booms old Mrs Peddie. The others wait, but it seems this is a final pronouncement. Old Mrs Peddie rarely catches the drift of general conversation, but has an uncanny knack of following important issues.

Grace faces the old lady squarely so her lips may be read. 'I have no right?' she asks. 'I have no right when it comes to Mildred's wishes?'

'This is nonsense!' Mrs Peddie shouts back. 'I am talking about rights!'

'But I simply asked . . . '

Mrs Peddie rolls on at top volume. 'Mildred Catherwood has no right to die just because it suits her. No. Imagine if it caught on! There have been many times it would have suited me . . .'

'Oh Mother . . .' says Cynthia. She smiles helplessly.

'Yes there have, dear. Many times. But we must struggle on and do our best. Mildred has a duty. I will go and tell her.'

'I'm afraid it will do no good, Mrs Peddie,' says Grace. 'I've spoken firmly to Mildred several times. She just lies there. I'm sure Les is right: it's a medical problem.'

But Mrs Peddie is adamant. She points a shaking finger in Grace's general direction. 'You're angry with her. Yes you are — pink cheeks, tight lips. Angry. But do you show your need? Dr Rama is a good doctor. If he says Mildred is simply depressed, she is. Try harder, girl, if you want her.'

There is a silence. Les looks at Grace and shrugs as if to say, How can you argue with this irrational old woman, but Grace looks away, feeling the weight, the sense, of Mrs Peddie's words.

'We must all try harder,' announces Mrs Peddie. It seems to be an order. 'Cynthia, you and I will visit Mildred tomorrow.' She picks up her handbag, a sign that she is ready for someone to move her.

But it is really up to me, thinks Grace that evening. She is watching the park as she often does. Her room grows dark while she stands, thinking about Mrs Peddie's words. Across the park, a light is on in Mildred's bedroom. The live-in nurse, provided by the family, has pulled the curtains.

I should go there now, thinks Grace. She is impatient with her tears. Her need for Mildred to live surprises her. Over the years she has accepted the deaths of her husband, her daughter and, recently, her dear friend Max. But the loss of Mildred's steady friendship, the fun they have together, seems quite unacceptable. Grace shakes her head in frustration. She cannot think what she might do or say to help Mildred turn the corner. If it were a rational argument over some issue of the day, Grace could be eloquent. But on matters of personal relationships words shy away from her. The language is simply not there.

All the same I will go now, decides Grace, and puts on her best blue coat.

Grace is shocked again at the way Mildred looks. Her body hardly raises a bump in the white coverlet. The nurse has brushed out her hair and it spreads over the pillow grey and lifeless. Mildred's cheekbones stand out. Her face is falling in on itself.

'See if you can get her to drink some tea,' says the nurse, 'or take a spoonful of soup. I can't do anything with her.' She pads out to the kitchen and the television.

Grace looks at Mildred. 'A bit starchy, that one,' she says. 'Not much fun, I imagine. You need a good laugh, Mildred.'

Mildred's eyes are half open but she is not looking at anything.

Grace feels desperate. 'Mildred.' A pause. 'Mildred, I need to say something to you but don't know how. Help me.'

Mildred sighs and her eyes move a little, not focusing but wandering in Grace's direction.

'Mildred, about Max. He's dead. He passed away, Mildred. I have been . . . oh . . . down in the dumps . . . There are things I should have said to you. You would have helped, but I never talked about him because I thought you disapproved. Perhaps,' Grace looks down; the words are hard, '. . . perhaps . . . Did you feel a little jealous? That he was breaking up our friendship? Mildred, I don't think he could have done that, even if he had lived.'

Grace pauses again. This time Mildred's eyes are sharper. She has not moved, but she watches Grace now.

'Oh Mildred, I feel silly talking like this. You are my dear friend. Don't die, please.' Grace reaches out and holds tight onto the frail white hand lying on the bed. It is possibly the first time she has touched Mildred. There is a response — a small pressure back.

Grace wants to weep with joy, but she will not let go her task. Fiercely she holds Mildred's attention.

'You've gone down the wrong path, Mildred. I need you here. It's not time for either you or me to go. Now. You must listen. Take a little soup and listen. I have some very interesting news!'

Mildred accepts a spoonful. And another. Every part of Grace's body is wound tight. All her energy streams towards Mildred. She has never worked so hard and the feeling is marvellous.

'You'll never believe, Mildred,' she says, 'what's going on at bowls. Les Comfrey is courting the French baker's mother!'

Grace gossips for all she is worth. Where she can't think of new scandals or surprises, she makes them up. She loses sense of time. Perhaps she has been performing for ten minutes, perhaps two hours. Every now and then she offers more soup. At a particularly outrageous assertion Mildred finally smiles.

'Oh now, Grace,' she says, 'surely you are making that up!' Her voice is faint but it is undeniably Mildred, back again.

Grace holds tight. 'Well, you'll just have to see for yourself,' she says.

At that moment there is a knock on the door. Grace hears the nurse murmuring to the visitor something about the late hour.

'It is life and death!' shouts old Mrs Peddie. 'What does time matter? Cynthia, take my arm!'

The old and the young Mrs Peddies advance into the

bedroom, Cynthia's gentle apologies crushed under her mother-in-law's onslaught.

'I felt I was needed,' booms the old lady. 'Mildred, I felt you slipping away.'

'Mother, take it gently, she's ill,' says Cynthia.

'What dear? Speak up!' shouts old Mrs Peddie. 'We must save Mildred!'

'Mrs Peddie,' says Grace, 'I think you'll find that already . . . '

Mrs Peddie ignores all diversions. She slumps onto the bed, causing a major earthquake. Mildred's flat body rises and falls in the shock wave. Old Mrs Peddie leans forward.

'Now Mildred, take a grip on yourself. You have no right to slip away like this. Grace here needs a friend. She's not been herself lately. What are you thinking of, leaving her alone like this? And what's more,' she adds, 'you have a great deal more to learn about laying down a good bowl.'

Grace smiles, letting the words flow. Her attention is still focused. She could not let go of Mildred's hand if she tried. Mrs Peddie settles herself more firmly on the bed; excitement is unbalancing her.

'It's not too hard,' she shouts. 'You'll get the knack of it.' Whether she means bowls or old age is not clear.

Grace feels the lovely bony fingers move, come to life, against her wrist as Mildred breathes in slowly.

'Thank you,' whispers Mildred to Grace.

'She spoke!' proclaims Mrs Peddie. 'Did you see that? Speak up, Mildred dear! What was that?'

Grace's eyes remain steady on Mildred's. 'She said thank you.'

Mrs Peddie applauds as they do at bowls when a good ball is sent up. 'Yes! I've done it! Brought her round! What did I tell you, Cynthia — effort is always rewarded. Now,' she pats Mildred's free hand vigorously, 'what about a game of Scrabble?'

'Oh Mother,' says Cynthia, 'don't be ridiculous. Mildred needs rest. It's time we went.'

'Nonsense, dear. I never retire before midnight. Or a drink, Mildred? A little drink to celebrate?'

Mildred's eyes rest on Grace. There is definitely a spark this time.

'Sherry?' she murmurs, 'Grace, you know where . . . '

Grace does not want to let go. She sighs, then gently lays her friend's hand down on the immaculate coverlet. Blood sings through her body as if some gate has been opened.

'We'll have a sherry to celebrate,' she says, speaking directly to Mildred, 'and then Mrs Peddie must go. I will stay the night here.'

As she stands, Grace bends to kiss Mildred's wasted cheek. 'Thank you,' she says.

'No, no. Glad to help,' shouts Mrs Peddie.

Mildred shifts slightly on the pillow. The grating, papery sound she makes could be a cough, but Grace recognises it as a first laugh.

Room by room Grace lights up the house as she goes to fetch the decanter.

Part Two

IN NEED OF A KEY

The odd person, walking dogs or children across the park, may look up and notice a tiny woman. Framed in the lower section of a double-hung sash, pale face, dark clothing, splash of yellow — a scarf perhaps? — she is so still, so formal, she could be a portrait, on display to the public. But it is Grace, looking out across the park, to Mildred's house. There, none of the usual morning signs are on display: bedroom curtain pulled back — signal that Mildred has showered and dressed; kitchen window open — Mildred has burnt the toast again; living-room blinds up — Mildred is on her morning round of housework. Like raising the flag on a parade ground, these are little reassurances to Grace that a new day is properly under way. Grace knows the house is empty, that her friend is in Christchurch visiting family, but her watching habit is too strong. She thinks, It's time I started a new project. But her thought lacks energy.

She remembers a lively argument on the beach with Max. 'You spend too much time *doing* and not enough *being*, my dear,' he had shouted above the waves. 'Conversations, friendships, have just as much validity as your projects.'

Grace had disagreed; had put the case for learning new skills, challenging the brain, always having work in hand.

'Yes yes, all that,' said Max, 'but in you, Grace, it's out of balance. You're a wonderful example of the puritan work ethic. How shall we open you out? Unlock you, share you around?'

Grace smiles, remembering Max's exuberance. How easily he had expanded her world; how difficult, now, to prevent it closing in. She looks again at Mildred's empty house. Mildred certainly shares herself around. Max would approve. And yet, she adds, in her own defence, Max and I made a good pair.

She sighs: a tiny movement. Grace knows she will always need a Max or Mildred to conduct her out, like electricity, towards others. Alone, her energy reverts to a closed circuit of self-contained activity. She becomes socially inert.

'Well, Mildred, I miss you,' says Grace out loud, 'but this is how I seem to be. There's no sense moping.'

The portrait disappears. Grace has moved to the telephone.

'I wish to purchase a second-hand computer,' she says.

January 26th 1994

Dear Mrs Grace Brockie,
May I ask permission formally to call you aunt? You're nothing of the sort, I know, but what other name would suit? No one calls people Mrs these days. Anyway I have no aunts or great aunts at all and would love to acquire one!

You probably don't even know I exist. I'm Max Friedmann's granddaughter. Martin is my dad. I want to say, Aunt Grace, that I think the way my parents treated you was just appalling. You should have been invited to the funeral. I'm not like them and have given up religion.

Anyway, one of the reasons I'm writing is to say that Mum and Dad have given me this lovely old brooch. They said Grandad gave it to you but you returned it when he died. I think that's just so sad. May I give it back, please?

I only saw Grandad twice this year. Once when I was home for the holidays. He told me about you so warmly, Aunt Grace, I feel I know you. There was this picnic he had planned as a surprise for you. Sparks of excitement flew out of his eyes — you know what I mean? The other time he was dead. I loved Grandad, he was the only good thing about our family. I want you to know that I think your romance with Grandad was *wonderful* and so *right*.

There's another reason for this letter which is rather cheeky so feel free to say no. I have just been accepted for Drama School! Isn't it great! My parents are livid.

I'll be coming to Wellington next month. Do you by any chance take boarders? Or would you like to? I promise not to play loud music and would be out most of the time. Perhaps you need someone to take out your rubbish and change light bulbs and that sort of thing. I could help to cheer you up too, you must be missing Grandad.

Please say yes, I'm dying to meet you.

But of course say no if it doesn't suit.

Yours,
Sally Friedmann

February 2nd, 1994

Dear Mrs Brockie,
Thank you for your kind note and the return of the brooch.

Last time we met was not a happy occasion; I hope we can put that behind us. There is no cause for friction between us, now that my father-in-law has passed on.

The funeral was a sad yet joyous occasion. I believe that even though Martin's father did not embrace Our Lord Jesus in this world, he may yet come to that faith in the afterlife. He was a strong-willed man but of course we loved him. We pray for his soul.

One or two of the family have suggested that it was unchristian of Martin and me not to include you in the funeral events. I would like you to understand my attitude to your 'friendship' with Max. Please believe that there was nothing personal about it. Nor was it entirely based on religious teaching.

In many ways my concern was for you. Max had no right to entice you into a relationship when he knew he was so ill. It was thoughtless and unkind and could only lead to unhappiness on your part. Max was concerned too much with his own enjoyment and too little with the welfare of others. Both Martin and I were worried that you would be hurt.

I hope your feelings did not develop to such an extent that you now feel bereaved, as we of the family do.

I would like to give you a little memento of Max. Not the brooch which has gone to my daughter. Is there some other little thing you fancy? A piece of crockery perhaps?

Martin and I will be in town next week for a church meeting. Perhaps we could call to deliver it. I believe in forgiveness, as I am sure you do too.

Yours sincerely,
Sheila Friedmann

February 6th, 1994

Dear Mrs Grace Brockie,
I have delayed rather too long writing to you and now am at a loss how to begin. I am Max Friedmann's son, Adam. Do you remember me? The lad in grey shorts and shirt who ran endless laps around the park? Perhaps not. There was nothing very special to remember. Mother and Dad were the interesting ones in our family.

My father may have mentioned me more recently. I am a solicitor; a partner with Lambourne McGill in Christchurch and modestly successful in my own field. But I won't bore you with that. My father had no interest in legal matters and perhaps you feel the same.

Mrs Brockie, I do not wish to intrude on private matters, but I became aware during my last visit to Dad that a 'friendship' had developed between you and my father. It seems Dad did not wish to share your relationship with me. In fact I would only have been happy for him.

Please accept my condolences. It is too late, I realise, to make amends for my family's treatment of you. I should not have allowed Martin and Sheila to have their way. People with strong views are hard to withstand, do you find that? Nevertheless I should have stood up for your inclusion at the funeral. We have denied you the opportunity to farewell my father properly. I apologise.

Would you be interested to receive a visit from me in a fortnight's time? I will be up overnight for a legal conference. I have none of my father's vivacity, I'm afraid, but will do my best to entertain you. Perhaps dinner at a restaurant?

I would like you to accept this little memento of him. It is not valuable, but my father enjoyed it. Perhaps you will too.

Please forgive me if this gift is offensive in any way. My father will probably have told you I am socially inept.

Yours sincerely,
Adam Friedmann

Monday 7th February

Dear Mildred,
I am besieged by Friedmanns! Like stray cats, three of them have suddenly appeared to lay gifts and guilts at my doorstep. I believe they feel sorry for me. A peculiar brand of arrogance don't you think? They have all received polite but distant letters by return mail. Max was a wonderful man but I have no desire to become confidante and problem solver to his whole family. Sheila, the daughter-in-law, was particularly obnoxious. She believes it was her duty to discourage friendship between Max and me. As if we were children in her care. I'm afraid my reply was very curt.

Your problems, my dear, are a different matter. Mildred, I do feel you should not make a decision hastily. Your daughter is quite right in one sense: she and her family can provide assistance and security for you. But so can your friends and neighbours here. Do you really want to leave your home and a lifetime of connections?

My advice is — wait till you are a little stronger before you make any decision to move permanently.

On the home front, your new gardener, I'm afraid, is not up to much. Did you check her qualifications? I had to point out to her that honesty was a weed. It has seeded all down your bank.

'Oh,' she said, 'it's very pretty, though. Some people like it.'

I assured her you did not, and watched to make sure she made a proper job of removing it. Well, you can't expect a gardener to be personally involved can you? My own frontage will be quite outstanding this year.

You will laugh at me, Mildred. Here I go again — I have bought a second-hand computer! It's time I learned the wretched technique. You can't write anything these days, it seems, without a screen in front of you. Well, I have to admit it is heavy going, but if all those secretaries can learn word processing, so can I. Not that I will ever give in to the present fad for communicating through the computer. Email, they're calling it. An ugly word. It will never catch on. The comfort of receiving good notepaper containing personal handwriting will prevail in the long run, mark my words. I know you will agree.

Cio-Cio San is missing you. I feed her regularly, but I am not a cat person as you so rightly point out. I wonder if she can be ill? A visit to the vet would be out of the question I'm afraid. Cio-Cio must be almost half my weight. Do vets make home visits for larger animals, I wonder?

Well, my dear, Cio-Cio isn't the only one missing you. Do not let Judith pressure you. There is a good case for your return. We both may manage independence for several more years. Dr Ramachandran says if a woman reaches seventy in good shape there's every reason these days for her to survive to ninety! The figures are lower for men, of course.

The Peddies and Les Comfrey send their regards. Les is hounding us to join in his latest letters-to-the-paper campaign — I'm too sick of it to bother you with the details. That man tries the patience of a saint — and I am definitely not one of that heavenly brigade! Old Mrs Peddie is as indestructible as ever. Think of her, Mildred: you will likely have fifteen more years of active life. Bowls will start again soon, and we are all hoping you will be at the opening.

Affectionately,
Grace

HONORARY GRAN

Grace, interrupted doing her housework, stands in the hall. She looks out through the door-panes to a grey, windswept sea. One hand holds the telephone a little distance away from her hearing aid. Even so, the wretched thing whistles. As she talks the duster in her free hand brings up a glow on the woodwork of her bookshelves.

'Grace Brockie,' she says firmly, ready to repel anyone soliciting anything.

'Is that you, Aunt Grace? Sorry to ring so early.'

'Who is that speaking, please?' Grace disapproves deeply of those callers — usually the young — who insist on launching into a conversation without first identifying themselves.

'It's me, Sally Friedmann!'

'Sally. Do you know what toll calls cost at this time of day?'

'No, I'm here. I'm in Wellington, Aunt Grace.'

Grace frowns. Her polishing hand moves more quickly. 'Would you like to call me Grace, perhaps?'

'Or Gran? You could be my honorary gran.' There is something too bright, too cheerful about this clear young voice.

'You have some objection to my name?' says Grace, tired now of this conversation and irritated by the squealing hearing aid.

'Sorry. No, it's lovely. Sorry, Aunt Grace. Grace.'

Grace lets a pause develop before she continues. 'Did you find suitable accommodation, Sally?'

'Um sort of. Well, that's what I'm ringing about.'

'You received my letter?'

'Yes. Yes, of course. Yes, I understand absolutely. It was rude to ask. The thing is . . . '

'Are you still there, Sally?'

'. . . Yes.'

Grace can hardly hear the voice. She believes Sally may be close to tears. Whatever the problem is, thinks Grace, I don't want to hear it. But remembering Max, she waits for Sally to continue.

'. . . Sorry. The thing is they've found me a flat but I can't move in for two weeks so I'm at the backpackers.'

'Well, that's good, Sally.'

'No it's not! It's not! I don't know anyone. They're noisy. This huge blond guy, doesn't speak English, he was drunk last night and tried to pick me up, and I'm afraid that tonight . . . ' Sally takes a sobbing breath and rushes on. 'Well, I thought maybe if I came up after Drama School and met you, and if you liked me, maybe you'd let me stay just till the flat . . . Grace? Are you still there?'

Grace sighs. 'Yes Sally. Would you like to have dinner with me tonight?'

'Really? Could I? I don't want to impose . . . Shall I bring fish and chips for both of us?'

Grace has to smile. The young have no idea. 'I'm still quite capable of cooking a meal, Sally.'

'I didn't mean . . . Sorry. I didn't mean . . . Well, I just thought you might have arthritic fingers, or osteoporosis and not be able . . . '

'Sally, I have both those disabilities and can still cook a meal. Do you like tuna fish pie?'

'Tuna fish pie? Grandad cooked me that once.' Her voice is a little uncertain.

Grace laughs out loud, the whistling in her ear forgotten. 'Did he indeed? You might find the original version more successful.'

'I'd love to come. Shall I bring my sleeping-bag? Then if you liked me perhaps I could . . .?'

'Why don't you do that,' says Grace. Already she is planning a pudding. Something hot. What do young people like these days?

'I don't mind the floor. And I'm quite small.'

'Sally, I have a full-sized spare bed. But I believe we should meet each other first. Have you considered that you might find me intolerable?'

'Grandad loved you.'

'Well. Max was different.'

'I will too, I just know I will.'

The young are so headstrong, thinks Grace; then she has a new thought. 'Sally, are you computer literate?'

'Yes of course.'

'Good. Excellent. Shall we say 6 pm?'

'You're quite a surprising person, Aunt Grace.'

'Pardon? I'm a little deaf.'

Sally's laugh sets off the hearing aid again. 'I think I'm going to like you — Grace!'

'Never judge character over the telephone, Sally, the impression is bound to be inaccurate. Let's make up our minds in the flesh, shall we?'

'Yes. Of course.'

Sally's voice is uncertain again. Grace would like to take back her little lecture. 'Take heart, Sally,' she says, 'even the most exciting new life is unsettling at first.'

'. . . Yes.'

'All right now?'

'Yes. Thank you. I'll see you tonight!'

'Please try to be on time. Goodbye.'

But Sally has already rung off.

As Grace puts fresh sheets on the bed, prepares food, lays the table, she tries to rationalise her feelings. Why this apprehension? Why this shrinking away from new contacts? Max would not approve. Mildred on the other hand would advise caution. Someone unknown, after all.

Grace puts out spoons and then good cloth serviettes. I'm neither Max nor Mildred, she thinks, and I'll have to find my own way. Perhaps if I think of Sally as a new project . . .

16th February 1994

Dear Mrs Brockie,
I understand my daughter is staying with you temporarily. Thank you for your kindness. Sally's temperament is not nearly as robust as she would like people to think. She has had health problems recently.

I would be grateful it you could let me know how Sally is. She rejects us completely at present. It is a phase, I trust, but meanwhile Martin and I hear nothing.

Drama School is not the right choice for Sally, we feel. We pray that she may turn towards a more acceptable career. Unhappily our family discussion on Sally's future became heated and Sally has not spoken to us since. Martin has his father's stubborn streak. It you are able to offer Sally some mature advice please take the opportunity.

I am sorry my earlier letter caused offence. We have different views; our Church exhorts us to consider the well-being of others. I hope you can respect my beliefs. I will try to understand yours.

May the Good Lord Jesus bless you for your hospitality. I miss my daughter, and am relieved she is with you.

Yours sincerely,
Sheila Friedmann

21st February

Dear Sheila,
Thank you for your letter, and for the box of citrus which arrived safely. I will see to it that Sally eats them all, never fear!

Sally is working hard and enjoying Drama School. Her studies leave her little time to get into mischief. I'm afraid I am not inclined to persuade her into a different career. Acting is an old and honoured profession. Perhaps your daughter has real talent. To be able to inspire audiences; to illuminate great plays — great truths — is a rare skill. If Sally has that skill, she should develop it, I feel.

Don't be hard on her, Sheila. Daughters often choose paths we cannot understand. Mine chose the worst possible path. At least your Sally is alive and doing something she believes in. One day surely she will return to her family.

I will certainly encourage her to write or ring you.

You say Sally has had health problems. Perhaps if I knew the nature of the problem, I could help her better?

Do not hesitate to write again.

Yours faithfully,
Grace Brockie

March 3rd

Dear Mrs Brockie,
Thank you for your letter. You are kind and mean well, but I am a little surprised you do not take our side over Sally's career. Our daughter is going through quite a wayward phase. She has been a great worry to us over the last two years. This experiment with the theatre is a real disappointment, especially with the love and forgiveness we and others at the Church have shown her.

Why can she not show the same care and respect that we have accorded her? During her years at University, Sally strayed. I will not go into details, but it was most painful. She returned to the Church, and Martin found her a decent job, but then, despite all our prayers, she strayed again. Now, her leaving the family to become an actress is like a slap in the face. It seems that she is deliberately setting out to hurt us. I know we must bear suffering cheerfully, but this is hard, and it would help if you supported our wishes.

You may not know that Sally's older brother, Tom, has gone to Australia and plays in a pop group. Tom is musical, like his grandfather, Max. We made sacrifices to make sure Tom's music teachers were the best, and now he has thrown it all back at us. Tom was to have continued in the family business. We have an orchard, mostly pip-fruit, and Martin also hires out picking equipment. Recently Martin bought another block in young trees which was to have been managed by Tom. Martin is devastated. And now Sally, who used to be the sensible one, has left us too. It is not right. Children should be a joy to their parents. At present our future seems bleak. I pray that Sally's heart will soften. Tom, I fear, is beyond redemption. You suggest that you have lost a daughter, Grace. You must understand how I feel.

You ask about Sally's health. It is somewhat confidential. What is past is past. Sally is weak willed and fell in with poor company. I am relieved to know that she is working hard and living in a sober home with you.

Martin is finding it hard to be charitable. He was proud of Sally. We both were. We hoped she would settle here, marry a good young man from the Church, and live a happy and fulfilled family life as we have. That hope is a shattered dream if Sally continues in the theatre. I can only wait and pray.

Please continue to send news meantime.

Yours faithfully
Sheila (Friedmann)

FEELING THE YEARS

Grace glares at the computer screen. The paragraph she is typing has suddenly disappeared. She stabs a finger at an arrow key. Her paragraph appears, rising, and continues upwards out of sight again. Grace explodes.

'This is ridiculous! Surely among all these functions, there is some slow-down button for learners?'

Sally laughs. 'Hey, this old software moves like a dinosaur as it is. Here.'

She leans over Grace's shoulder, touches keys lightly and Grace's memoirs settle down meekly in the centre of the screen. It is almost more than Grace can bear.

'Wait. Show me!' But Sally is off down the hall, singing, to make coffee. Grace types on. For two weeks she has wrestled with her wretched computer. She can now sit in front of a screen and sometimes make the beast bend to her will. But more often the mouse, the keys or some other part of the machine seem to have a life of their own. This piece of hardware, making too much of itself in her comfortable old study, is a tough nut to crack. Grace is not used to failure. In the past decade she has studied leatherwork, Spanish, the political history of Bosnia-Herzegovina, Thai cooking, car maintenance and comparative systems of proportional representation. All these she has grasped on her own, at home, from books, manuals and teaching tapes. For Grace, gathering new information is an addiction.

Don't you dare!' Grace speaks to her text which has suddenly split into two camps, moving steadily in different directions.

The *concept* of computer technology is not the problem. Grace loves systems. Jane Austen has been replaced on the bedside table by the unbelievably bulky WordPerfect manual, and Grace, though deeply disapproving of the language, has understood and memorised many sections.

No, if mastering the computer were all theory, Grace would be steaming along quite nicely by now. Her body is the culprit. Grace's old fingers, familiar with an Olivetti, will not learn; cannot manage a soft touch. The brisk way she strikes the keys fills Sally with horror. Grace likes to pause, gaze out at the trees, reflecting on the suitability of a word. Her hands rest comfortably on the keyboard. When the decision is made, the perfect phrase selected, Grace returns to the screen to find pages of nonsense are spreading like a plague over her careful document.

Grace growls as a set of instructions appear, uninvited and flashing as if warning of imminent disaster. The computer has succeeded in making her feel old.

'Grace,' says Sally, returning just in time to correct the error with casual speed, 'Was it Sophocles who wrote *Trojan Women*?' She plonks a cup of coffee on top of the hard drive; a computer is simply another piece of furniture to Sally.

'Euripides,' Grace corrects, and leans back, ready to discuss Greek tragedy, but Sally has gone again.

Later Sally, crosslegged on the couch, flicking through old photograph albums, announces she will be leaving tomorrow; the space in her flat is now vacant.

'I'll miss you, Sally,' says Grace, and means it. This complex young woman fascinates her. Vivacious like Max, but, unlike him, romantic and vulnerable, Sally will make a fine actor, Grace suspects. Her presence in the house has been both an irritation and an illumination. Dusty, unvisited corners of Grace's life have been explored, lit by Sally's relentless curiosity. Grace, at first resisting these probes into her past, has grown to enjoy them. If only Sally didn't dart around so! In an instant Sally, terrierlike, will sniff at a story, shake it sharply to see what falls out and then discard the morsel for meatier bones. Grace and Mildred would have settled in for hours.

Was I once like this, Grace wonders; have I slowed down so much, or are young people today just faster? Perhaps computer literacy is mutating them.

'Is this your daughter?' says Sally. 'Look at her nose — just like mine!' Sally presents her quite different profile. 'Grace, you and Grandad — did you by any chance . . .?'

Grace laughs. Two weeks ago she would have let a disapproving silence develop. 'All you share with my daughter is a vivid imagination, Sally. You won't unearth anything juicy. Max and I were good, very good, friends.'

'You loved each other!'

'Yes, Sally. We did.' Grace can say it easily now. She cannot explain what a joy it has been to talk about Max; to have their love accepted, probed, laughed over. These two weeks have unravelled a knot: Sally has allowed Grace, at last, to farewell Max.

'Have you written to your mother?' she asks, knowing the answer.

'Written?' Sally does not share Grace's respect for letter-writing. 'They only live an hour and a half away.'

'Sheila called today with lemons and a cake. I suspect it was an excuse. She wants to see you.'

'She wants to persuade me into a respectable career!'

'I can't imagine anyone having much of a chance against you in an argument.'

'Oh it's different with you. You're rational. Their ideas have set like concrete ages ago. You can't argue against them. I lose my temper or storm out.'

'Well you must find a way of dealing with it, Sally. Sheila's your mother, and always will be.'

In fact Grace found herself warming to the stolid woman in her plain dress and headscarf, standing awkwardly on the porch. Once, standing in Max's kitchen, wearing Max's pyjamas, Grace was intimidated by the arrival of Sheila. This morning, suitably dressed, and on her own territory, Grace could afford to be hospitable.

Sheila was eager for news of her daughter; it gratified Grace to be able to give it. Once or twice, in the course of conversation, Grace came up hard against the rock of Sheila's narrow beliefs, but in the sunny kitchen, over a cup of real coffee and a piece of Sheila's cake, Grace felt disposed to skirt the obstruction.

With Max, now, thinks Grace, it would be different. She remembers the sharp enjoyment of their arguments. Or am I simply losing my edge?

'Hey, look at this!' says Sally. 'Front page of the *Evening Post*! That's you and Gillian! You were famous!'

Grace is able to smile. 'My daughter was very talented. For a brief time well known, I suppose. I was just her mother.'

Sally looks up from the album and considers Grace. 'You look quite different in the photograph. Much younger.'

'I *was* much younger.' Nevertheless Grace frowns. Too many times today she has felt aware of her age. She doesn't expect to. For the past twenty years she and Mildred have considered an old person to be someone about ten years ahead. Today the gap has telescoped. Grace blames the computer.

Sally is watching her closely. Bony knees under her chin, dark eyes alert, she is intent on dragging out secrets. Then with a flinging of limbs, she is up and leaning over the back of Grace's chair.

'I'll miss you, Grace,' says Sally, planting a kiss on the top of the grey head. 'Can I come up now and then for a proper meal?'

'You can indeed, but not unannounced. I enjoy planning something special.'

'Great! Could I bring a friend sometimes?'

'We'll see about that. And don't think,' adds Grace, severity spicing her pleasure, 'that the odd balanced meal here will keep you healthy. An actor needs a sound body, not one stuffed with junk food!'

'"Fie, Fie! unknit that threatening unkind brow, and dart not scornful glances from those eyes,"' says Sally.

'Katherine, *Taming of the Shrew*, last scene,' says Grace, and adds, '"Be thou familiar but by no means vulgar."'

'From the same speech?'

'Not even the same play. You should know *Hamlet*.'

Sally throws up her hands in surrender. 'Is there anything you don't know? Your head beats a computer any day. You're a walking reference library, Grace.'

As she prepares for bed Grace pauses in front of the mirror. She nods approval, realising that the threshold for old age has receded to its proper place — somewhere around the ninety mark.

Perhaps I will pay Sally to type my notes, thinks Grace. The poor girl needs money.

She picks up Jane Austen.

March 12th 1994

Dear Mrs Friedmann,
I have just discovered that you have entered into a correspondence with my wife over our daughter, Sally.

Sally has deliberately, with forethought, walked away from her family. Until she, of her own volition, in a proper frame of mind, returns, I do not wish anyone in our family to have contact with her. We forgave her blatant experiments with alcohol. We even forgave her for terminating a new life. Time and again we welcomed her back into the Church. Now it is her turn to make the first move.

Sheila and I would rather not hear news of Sally until she has made her own peace with us.

Yours,
Martin Friedmann

encl: Cheque for $200. Sally will not be paying you adequately for her board.

March 26th

Dear Martin and Sheila,
Perhaps you will destroy this letter without opening it. I hope not. Such extreme behaviour is surely not called for. Sally is simply doing what every son or daughter does — finding her own way in the world.

Think of your own family history, Martin. You certainly did not follow Max and Ilona's path. Perhaps they were disappointed you gave up music. They certainly found it difficult to accept that when you married Sheila, you embraced her religion. It is not for me to undermine your faith, but you must admit its unbending moral codes do not welcome those of us who are outside. Yet Max and Ilona kept on patiently with their love and acceptance of you both. Sally is simply breaking out of her family mould, as you did, Martin. Your pattern, Sheila, may have been the same.

I do not feel inclined to cease writing to you, as you request. Perhaps I'm foolish; my arguments may never be read. But it is something I must do. You will remember Gillian's death, Martin. In some ways I failed my daughter. I do not intend to fail another young woman who is at a crossroads. I hope, sincerely, that you do not fail her either.

Sally no longer boards with me. She flats with three other quite presentable acting students. Once a week she eats a proper meal here with me. She seems active and busy, though a little homesick, I believe.

Please keep communication open with Sally. I'm sure you both mean a great deal to her, despite her stubborn independence. I have become very fond of her; you have a sensitive and intelligent daughter.

I am returning the cheque. Sally paid me quite adequately.

Yours faithfully,
Grace

Wednesday March 30th

Dear Grace,
Your last letter made Martin very angry. He destroyed it.

I do not wish to be the cause of friction between my husband and me. It is not right. Martin is a good man and a good husband.

I will not seek further news of Sally. She has turned her face from us. We must wait patiently till she sees reason. I pray for her every day.

My visit to you was weakness. I confessed everything to Martin. He was kind and understanding but we both agree I must try to be stronger. Thank you for making me so welcome. And for looking after Sally. Your actions have been kindly meant, I am sure, but Martin and I would prefer that you avoid further contact with our daughter. She is easily seduced by Liberalism and Wayward Thoughts. Left to her own devices she may begin to reflect on the advantages and comforts of family and Church.

I enclose some literature about our Church and its teachings. It may help you to a greater knowledge of our beliefs. There is great joy in following the path of Jesus and the teachings of the Holy Bible. You will not find anywhere in the Good Book references to a woman's place being to entertain the general public by acting on the stage.

Yours sincerely,
Sheila

P.S. Martin has certainly not given up his music. He is organist for our congregation and a respected choirmaster.

PERFORMING GENES

'I'm chucking it in,' says Sally. Her voice is almost too low for Grace to hear.

Sally's elbows are propped on the bench. Shoulders hunched, she stares down into the gully.

'You don't need to look at me like that,' she says. 'It's my life.' Grace continues to look. She is trying to make up her mind whether this is a serious statement, or simply a moody moment. Serious, she decides. Usually there is an element of teasing in Sally's moods; of watching to see what effect she's having. Today, Sally's announcement is flat. It doesn't invite response.

'Is there something particular the matter, Sally?' Grace thinks she can detect a greyness in the skin, a downward drag of the body. 'Have you been eating properly?'

Sally looks at Grace sharply, but doesn't answer. She turns her back to Grace as if hiding something.

'Would you peel these potatoes then?'

Grace believes activity is the best cure for depression. She puts bowl, peeler and potatoes down in front of the drooping girl. Grace rattles in the saucepan cupboard for a bit, then settles to making pastry. Her old hands spread flour, knead and shape the dough. She waits.

Slowly the grey peelings fall into the bowl. Sally rinses one naked potato and lays it on the bench. She runs a finger over its glistening surface. After a while she picks up another potato. As her hands fall into the rhythm, the words come.

'I'm no good at it, that's all. I haven't got it.'

'What makes you think that?'

'They told me.'

'I'm sure they didn't! And who is they, might I ask?'

'The tutors. We did impros. Mine was ratshit.'

'Don't expect me to understand your jargon, Sally. Plain English will do.'

'And yesterday I bombed out in singing. I'm just not going to make it.'

Gradually Grace pieces together the chain of disasters. Sally presented an improvisation but could tell it fell flat. She was badly knocked by her tutor's criticism. Then a demanding singing lesson had resulted in tears. The final blow, it seems, is that Felix, her flatmate, has dropped her.

'I wasn't aware he'd picked you up,' says Grace, who is not comfortable with these casual references to relationships.

'We were sort of an item. Well, I thought so. Anyway I'm leaving. There's no point spending two years hard slog to end up a failure.'

Sally slices a potato fiercely, and cuts again. They will cook too quickly, but Grace holds her peace; the anger is a good sign.

'I'm not going home, though. And don't you tell Mum and Dad. I know you write to them. I couldn't stand their smug I-told-you-sos.' Sally is crying now, trying to hide it.

'Sally,' says Grace, her heart aching for this homesick young woman, 'would you get me some mint, please?'

She watches Sally clump down the steps to the garden. The wind blows the girl's dark hair over her face. Her loose shirt swirls and flaps. For a moment, in the buffeting, the figure blurs, loses its definition. Grace is alarmed. Sally is drifting, and Grace is unsure what anchor might usefully tether her. She sighs impatiently over Martin and Sheila. Their intransigence is an unaffordable luxury. Sally needs their support. It would be easier all round if Sally chose a different career and yet acting seems to lighten her. On good days Sally almost flies. Grace wants to persuade her to stay at Drama School.

She frowns at the knock on the door. This is not the moment for interruption.

Standing against the light is an unfamiliar figure. He is a thin young man, tall, slightly stooped, with something strange on his head.

'Hi. I'm Tom Friedmann. Is my sister here?'

Grace, taken aback, motions him inside. In the light the thing on his head is revealed as extremely surprising hair. A high crest of peroxide curls sweeps from his forehead over the top of his head and down to his shoulder blades. The rest of his head is shaved and gleams as if oiled. The boy is aware of his impression and stands taller. He smiles; Grace catches a flicker of Max around the eyes.

'They said at the flat Sally was here. Is she?'

'Tom.' Grace swallows. She wonders whether she is about to be robbed, or worse. Sally is enough on her own, thinks Grace, without this weird brother — if indeed he is related. She motions him inside and shuts the door firmly.

'Sally is down in the kitchen. She is rather upset. Perhaps you could cheer her up?'

The tall young man grins down at her; then nods as if Sally upset is a condition familiar to him. 'Which way?'

Grace follows Tom down the hall. He pads along easily, swinging his hips, looking from side to side at pictures and books as he goes. Grace wants to touch the rioting crest. He looks like Achilles at the walls of Troy. His collarless once-white shirt hangs long over scruffy purple trousers. The general effect is rather splendid in a tired sort of way. Grace frowns at the dirty sneakers and odd socks.

In the kitchen Sally is chopping mint without enthusiasm.

'Hi Sis!' says the Greek god. Sally spins round. The shock dries her eyes. Her puffy face goes white, then redder than ever.

'Tom!' she wails. Her minty fingerprints add to the marks on his shirt, and the tears flow again. The brother wraps long arms around her, patting her shoulder as if she were a small animal. 'Hey . . . hey . . . ' he says, looking across to Grace for assistance.

What an unmatched pair, she thinks. Tom's gangly grace and Sally's tightly knit little body seem to have come from different planets. 'Perhaps,' she suggests, 'we all need a drink. What about a glass of sherry?'

'Sherry,' says Tom. There is a pause. 'I don't suppose you'd have a beer?' Sally makes a muffled noise into Tom's shoulder.

'I do not,' says Grace, 'but there's a very nice lemon and mint cup in the fridge. My own recipe.'

'Way to go,' says Tom. 'Sounds like my number. I've got a throat like a stag's roar.'

Grace assumes this means yes. Sally talks with her brother as Grace sets out glasses and cake.

'I tell you what,' says Tom, 'you wouldn't have enough for the band, would you? We've been on the road all day.'

It turns out three others are waiting in the van outside. A lime green plastic doll is impaled on the aerial and a rash of golden daisies, probably concealing rust spots, dance over the bodywork. NIGHT SCENTED STOCK is painted in a blood-red diagonal slash over doors and windows. The interior seems crowded with bodies and equipment.

'Night Scented Stock,' says Tom proudly, 'the name of our

band.' Grace wants to ask why such a beautiful delicate flower should be chosen to represent a pop band, but already Tom is shouting down for all the street to hear, 'Hey guys! Pit stop!'

Grace watches in apprehension as doors burst open and three other purple and white apparitions come up her path. All are peroxide blondes, the girl's hair short, like velvet, showing the delicate bones of her head, the two boys different versions of nightmare.

Max, Max, thinks Grace, this is too much. But the thought of Max, laughing at her discomfort, urging her to enjoy life's oddities, unties the knot all the same.

Around the kitchen table the Night Scented Stock become ordinary hungry members of the human race. A whole cake is devoured; Grace opens a biscuit tin and is toasted in lemon mint cup. As he demolishes ginger crunch, one of the boys drums with grubby fingernails on the back of a chair. He is in a different private world, answering in indecipherable monosyllables to equally strange questions. Grace realises that turning up her hearing aids will make no difference. The one who looks Maori or Polynesian and seems to be called Dambo shrugs himself upright, smiles politely at Grace then peers down at the garden, humming to himself. The drummer asks him a question and he answers over his shoulder, casually. The chat goes back and forth over and around Grace, but in a desultory, disconnected way that seems alien. She wants to sit them down and ask clear questions — get a good conversation going.

The peroxide velvet girl has sat slumped and sullen in a corner during the feast, crumbling her cake in a manner that irritates Grace, who can't tell whether the girl is unhappy or simply disengaged. She seems so different from Sally, whose moods are fierce and open for all the world to read. Grace tries to bring the withdrawn girl to life. 'Why,' she asks, 'do you call your band after a flower?'

The girl frowns at her fingernails. Her muttered reply could mean anything. Her only show of animation comes when Sally mentions Drama School. 'Hey wow!' she says, 'Drama School! I auditioned three times and never even got shortlisted. You must be awesome.'

'That's my sis,' says Tom. 'We're a performing family, eh Sal? Skipped a generation, but genes are survivors.'

Grace hears this and laughs at the boy's arrogance.

'You young people! Isn't your father musical, Tom?'

'Come off it! We're talking music here. Dad plays a church organ, for Christ's sake. Square little dinky four-line verses. Colourless rubbish.'

Grace frowns. She is unwilling to align herself with Martin and Sheila, but the desire to argue is too strong.

'Surely church music, hymns, are relevant to some? I enjoy music, but not your sort. Does that make me unmusical?'

Tom considers. He cocks his crest on one side and grins at Grace.

'Not unmusical. Just uneducated. I like Bach and Stravinsky. Listen to them if the mood is right. You probably haven't applied yourself to pop. Eh?'

'It is hard to be unaware of pop these days . . . '

'And I'll bet my sweet butt you don't listen properly. Have you ever paid careful attention to — say — Miles Davis? Pink Floyd? The Beatles? Classics, all of them.'

Grace is relieved The Beatles are mentioned. Otherwise she would not have the faintest idea what he is talking about. 'One or two of the Beatles' songs . . . ' she begins, but then cannot continue. What is there to say about them? 'Quite catchy,' she finally manages.

Tom taps a bony finger on the kitchen table. He is enjoying himself. 'Catchy,' he repeats wagging his crest at her, 'much more than catchy. Harmonically, the best of The Beatles' numbers are up there with Bach.'

Grace snorts. 'Surely not. You're overstepping there, young man. Bach has survived for centuries. Will your Beatles?'

Tom nods, sure of himself. 'I'd lay a bet on it.' He turns away, adding a comment to one of the others and Grace misses the drift. She feels alive, though. It has been some time since she crossed verbal swords with anyone. It is clear to her that Max passed on more than musical genes to this articulate boy. The other band members are self-absorbed drifters in comparison.

Tom drapes a long arm over his sister's shoulder, 'By the way, message from Felix. You've got it all wrong. Whatever that means.'

The sun rises in Sally's face. 'He say why?'

'Nope. We're going to crash in your flat tonight, if it's cool with you?'

'Sure.' Sally's feet tap out a jazzy little routine.

Tom approves. 'But hey, what about this! We need another vocalist. Ariadne's ditching us. You'd earn a bit more than Drama School.'

Ariadne snorts and slouches lower on her chair. The drummer with the thousand grubby golden plaits looks sideways at Sally, slowly shaking his head. He mumbles something Grace takes to be negative.

'Yeah,' says Dambo, whose ponytail, bound with silver, stands proud and equine from his head; Grace expects him to whinny.

Tom is undaunted. 'Sal's got a voice to kill for. Come on, Sal, give us a number.' He looks round for electric points. 'We could set up in here — at a pinch — and give you a trial. If that's okay of course?' Tom looks at Grace with an easy charm that reminds her of his grandfather.

Sally rescues Grace. 'You've got to be joking, Tom. I know how long a set-up takes. And what will this proper neighbourhood think, once Jaz gets away on the drums?'

'Yeah well, only an idea . . . '

'And anyway, I'm going to be an actor. Bands are your thing.'

Sally smiles at Grace; a complicated crinkled look that says I've been an emotional fool, and I'm back on my perch now. Grace acknowledges the look. She is amazed at Sally's mercurial changes of mood. Surely we were more deliberate about life's important decisions, she thinks. Then remembers her own decision to be a teacher, against the wishes of her parents. She had been sitting with two friends on a sand dune watching cars racing over the beach. This was in the days before racing circuits or custom-designed racing cars. The beautiful elegant motors roared over the wet sand, their drivers, scarves streaming behind, laughing like gods. Grace and her friends were shrieking with excitement, hanging onto each other with mock terror. Grace's friend Adele turned shining eyes to the others and said, 'Let's not break up — let's all go to T. Coll together.' And so the decision was made, with no forethought, and the direction of Grace's life was laid down. It was the right decision too. Perhaps right choices are easy to make; it's the wrong ones we agonise over.

Grace wants to discuss this with Sally, but there is no chance.

The noise level is rising. They are all relaxing, settling down, it seems, for a long session. Grace is isolated in an unknown sea of jargon and laughter. She wonders if Night

Scented Stock will understand when it is time to go.

Sally understands. She rounds them up, demands to be transported back to her flat, demonstrates how she can squeeze inside an upturned drum for the short trip. Dambo holds Grace's hand and bows his head over it in an old-fashioned show of respect and Grace, now that they are going, can afford to be motherly and warm.

'Good luck for the rest of your tour,' she says, smiling as they burst outside and horse their way down the path. She draws the line at inviting them back though.

The noisy blond collection crams into the van, calling thanks to Grace. Sally gives a quick hug.

'Thanks. I love you.'

'Sally. Are you all right?' says Grace. She can still detect an unexplained shadow under the skin.

Sally hesitates, starts to speak, but Tom calls from the van.

'Move it, Sal, weren't you the one keen to get away?'

'Yeah yeah.' The moment has gone and Sally, knees and elbows in all directions, is arranged on top of everyone.

'Sally, is this wise? Surely it's against the law . . . ' But the door slams and the van toots up the road.

Alone in her suddenly bereft kitchen, Grace longs, with a sharp need, for Mildred. Wouldn't they laugh together. Wouldn't Mildred enjoy, and be terrified over the story of the peroxide band in Grace's kitchen?

I'll have the sherry anyway, thinks Grace. But in the end she doesn't pour; it's not the same.

As she begins her careful routine, preparing for bed, Grace wonders what stories Mildred might be needing to tell. Young people, families, are endlessly interesting, but an old friend has a warmer, steadier glow. Surely Mildred cannot make the break? Grace decides to write again tomorrow.

MUSES

Grace, tucked in bed, frowns at the telephone. There is warmth in the frown, though. Only chaotic Sally would ring at this time.

'Grace Brockie.'

'Hi!'

'Who is speaking, please?'

'Come on! You know it's me!'

'Sally, the considerate procedure is to identify yourself immediately. It's a habit you should acquire.'

'This is Sally Friedmann, first-year drama student speaking.'

'Good evening, Sally. Have you any idea what time it is?'

'Yes, I'm sorry but we're having this argument and I told them you'd know. Anyway your phone is by the bed and you read way past this time. Now, how many muses were there? Nine, right? Felix reckons three.'

'Usually nine, yes.'

'Ha! Felix, I told you!'

'But in early Greek times they worshipped three, I believe. Felix has a point.'

'You know too much! I'll stick with the nine. Can I come on Thursday? I need to talk.'

'Lovely. I missed you last week.'

'Yes, sorry. Something came up. Hey stop it, Felix!'

Amid giggles and protestations, the line goes dead.

SPELL-CHECK

This time it is Grace who waits anxiously for Sally to answer.

'Hi.'

'This is Grace Brockie speaking. Is Sally Friedmann available?'

'Didn't you recognise my voice, Grace?'

'Sally my dear, it's simply good manners . . . '

'I'm only teasing. Sally here, may I help you?'

'I certainly hope so. Have you a moment?'

'Of course I have. How are you?'

'In a worried state. Sally the whole document has disappeared.'

'The whole thing?'

'All sixty-seven pages. I was trying to correct your spelling and the screen suddenly went blank.'

'Oh dear. Where are you now?'

'In front of the wretched thing.'

'Try pressing F1.'

'An F and a one?' Grace searches for the keys.

'No! No! Stop! Up at the top of the keyboard, Aunt Grace.'

'Oh yes. Those. F1?'

'F1.'

'But soft, behold! Lo where it comes again!'

'*Hamlet*!'

'Today, Sally, you are invincible. Thank you, thank you.'

'F1 worked, right?'

'This is pure magic. How did you know?' Grace frowns at the docile page of writing. 'What is this F1, then, Sally? Clearly I need to know its function.'

'Aunt Grace? Save the document, exit and don't touch it again till I get there, right?'

'Well, you might be right. Save. Now where is it again?'

'The little square symbol, just under edit.'

'Oh yes.' Grace sighs. How is it that her memory seems to evaporate as soon as she sits in front of the computer? Some sort of radiation poisoning perhaps? Can the brains of the entire human race be plummeting? But look at Sally — sharp as needles when in front of the wretched thing. Even now Grace can hear the smile in her voice.

'There's a spell-check in the computer you know Aunt Grace. I would have done all that when I finished typing.'

'Soon there will be nothing left to learn at school.'

'True. Except how to control a computer. And anyway, is good spelling so important? Look at Shakespeare. Chaotic speller, and a genius.'

'Ah. There's an argument. But we'll save it, I think. I need all my concentration to tuck away this document. Bless you my dear, you shall have lemon meringue pie on Thursday. You are coming?'

'Ahh . . . yes. Yes. Sorry about last Thursday.'

'I thought you needed to talk, Sally.'

'Well, I did. I do. But I've got to sort it myself, really.'

'Are you in trouble?'

'Look, I just don't want to talk about it, okay?'

'Are you sure?'

'Sure.'

'Well, I can respect that. But surely if you wish to break a dinner engagement, it's good manners to ring and postpone?'

'Oh leave me alone!'
Grace looks at the receiver in astonishment.

OUT OF DEPTH

Grace lets the discussion roll on, waiting for a chance to bring up her problem. Most in the bowls club are more experienced with young people than she is, might well be able to offer advice, yet she is reluctant to expose her need. Finally, when Les Comfrey is advising Jack Chan on the correct recipe for a good concrete, Grace takes Cynthia Peddie aside and mentions Sally.

'She simply walked into the house, tears streaming down, went to bed and slept for fifteen hours.'

'How is she now?'

'Asleep again. Ate a good meal, cried again, and went back to bed. What do you think?'

'Overwork,' says Cynthia, 'Too much of everything, I expect.'

Grace agrees. 'There's no temperature. An appetite of sorts is there. She just seems so down.'

'Or boy trouble. That's often at the root of things.'

Grace smiles, remembering Sally's last depression. 'Perhaps.'

'If it's boy trouble stay out of it. Advice from our age group is never appreciated.' Cynthia frowns. 'They think experiences were so different back in our Dark Ages . . . Children can be so arrogant.'

Grace senses a story behind Cynthia's uncharacteristic outburst, but her concern over Sally is stronger than her curiosity.

'Yet I don't feel it's boy trouble this time.'

Old Mrs Peddie is not listening. Her new walking frame is a challenge when it comes to bowling and she is getting in a little extra practice during afternoon tea. The rest of the group are dividing their attention between Grace's problem and the possibility that Mrs Peddie will need urgent rescue.

Shirley Chan has been listening and now joins the conversation. 'Have you rung her parents?' she asks. 'There may be some history of depression.'

This is the nub of the problem for Grace. She needs reassurance from her friends.

'Sally was absolutely adamant that I shouldn't ring them. Quite hysterical. In the end, I promised not to. Was I right?'

'No, Grace,' says Shirley, 'the parents have a right to know. If Sally is really ill . . .'

'But she doesn't seem to be. And she's no longer a child.'

'Even so. You're trying to replace the role of the parent.' Grace feels this is a little unfair. It was Sally's idea, after all, to recuperate on Grace's spare bed. And yet guilt clouds her enjoyment of the nursing role.

'You think I should go against Sally's wishes?'

'Yes.' Jack obviously finds a human problem more interesting than concrete. He is just as definite as his wife on this matter. Grace suspects that Mildred would say the same if she were here. This could be a chance for reconciliation between Sally and her parents, yet Sally was so panicked at the thought.

Old Mrs Peddie staggers. A bowl has become trapped among the prongs of her walking frame. Les Comfrey hurries over but cannot control the toppling weight. Jack and Cynthia add their strength and equilibrium is reached. Old Mrs Peddie is indignant.

'You have to let me find my own way,' she booms, 'or I'll never learn. There's quite an art to this, but I'm getting the hang. Now who's for another head?'

'Mother,' says Cynthia, 'I think we've finished for today.'

'Nonsense, dear. I'm not the only one who needs extra practice. Les was in very poor form today.'

Les shakes his head at this impertinence, but turns to Grace.

'I think you'll find it's an abortion,' he says.

Everyone looks at Les in amazement. He turns slowly pink, but persists.

'Sally.' Les clears his throat. 'I think you'll find I've got my facts right. An unwanted pregnancy.'

There is a silence. The surprise is that Les would even mention such a topic. The question hangs in the air. Les turns pinker. He is desperately embarrassed, but bravely continues.

'Well, it's all in the past. I . . . knew someone. It was in the days before it was easy. But she did what she had to. Went to bed and cried. Terrible depression.'

Everyone hangs on Les's words. For once, thinks Grace, Les has the floor and would rather his audience was not so attentive.

Again it is old Mrs Peddie who creates a diversion.

'Well if no one wants to play, I'm going home!' she cries. Her walking frame clumps across the wooden floor with the old lady uncertainly ensconced. Cynthia laughs in some despair.

'It's me who has to get used to this frame,' she says. 'Suddenly Mother is independent again.'

'Cynthia!' Old Mrs Peddle has halted and is banging the frame about at the bottom of the steps. 'Do pay attention. This wretched device doesn't go up stairs! We shall have to take it back.'

Getting her up the stairs takes all of them. Nothing will induce Mrs Peddie to release her grip on the frame so the whole collection must be manoeuvred at once.

'There's no end to challenges at our time of life,' says Grace.

'Thanks dears!' cries Mrs Peddie, 'I'll practise on the garden steps before next bowls day.' Cynthia sends an alarmed look back at Grace as she tries to steer her mother-in-law towards the right car.

Les's gleaming station wagon is parked next to Grace's little Honda. He is hovering, still wanting to talk. Grace smiles.

'That can't have been easy, Les, talking about your own past like that. Thank you.'

Les opens his mouth in a gasp. He draws his stocky little body up.

'Grace, I would have thought you'd know me better than that! Surely you don't think . . . ' Les manages to show both outrage and a certain coquettish pride that anyone should consider him capable getting a woman in trouble.

Grace looks at Les with clear eyes. 'Les, if you have any advice to give on this matter, I'd be pleased to hear it.'

Suddenly Les is less sure of himself. He tells Grace of the time his daughter became pregnant to her employer — a married friend of the family. Les and his wife had been dreadfully upset; tried to hush the matter up. Against their daughter's wishes Les had arranged for her to go into the country to have the baby. Adoption was the only conceivable solution. Both parents wanted Jennifer out of the house as quickly as possible. Jennifer ran away and found someone to give her an abortion. Poor, pompous Les hesitates several times as he speaks. He is trying to appear matter-of-fact and in control but cracks are showing. Grace is touched that Les would expose himself so, in order to help her solve a problem. I do not deserve these good friends, she thinks.

'We tracked her down in the end,' says Les. 'Say what you like, Grace, but I blame the man. That was the last time he crossed our doorstep. Well, Jennifer was wrong too, I'll grant you that; coming between a man and his family. But in the end she was our blood and we couldn't cast her out.' His little round eyes are asking for Grace's acceptance. Grace smiles back. He has no idea, she thinks.

'She was in a hotel bed, crying — like your Sally. Didn't come out of that depression for three years. I don't mind saying, Grace, my wife had a hard time of it. Jennifer still won't forgive me for my part in the whole episode. After fifty years! She's quite irrational about it. My advice is, be careful how you deal with Sally, Grace. You're fond of her, I can see.'

Grace reaches out and gives Les a little pat. 'You're a good man despite all your reactionary views.'

'Reactionary! You simply never recognise good sense when you hear it. I know my facts, Grace . . .'

Grace opens her car door, turns back to him. 'Sometimes, Les, you do. Thank you. Yes. I'll take care with Sally.'

But as Grace buckles up, the mild sense of panic returns. I'm out of my depth here, she thinks. It is a rare sensation. She longs for Mildred's return.

May 5th

Dear Grace,
Thank you so much for accompanying me to dinner last week. I do hope you were not too bored. You are very kind to put up with me. My conversation is not up to much. The food was excellent, though, wasn't it?

I am taking up your suggestion that we correspond from time to time. Legal documents are more my stock in trade, but it will be good for me to try a lighter vein.

Well, I have been sitting here for half an hour wondering what on earth would interest you. Perhaps if I describe where I live?

My flat is four storeys up in a small apartment block overlooking Hagley Park. I think you would like it. I have one or two good New Zealand paintings — small ones, my flat is not large. And quite an extensive collection of CDs. Opera is my speciality. Did I tell you that I am a Friend of the Opera down here?

From my little balcony I can see the Alps, which are covered in snow at this time of year. Though you have to peer through my Chinese bamboo which is outgrowing its pot. I must prune it but somehow cannot bear to. It is so delicate and vulnerable!

There are two bedrooms, one converted into a little workshop. My hobby is to collect antique guns. Or, more properly, to refurbish them. At the moment I am reconstructing a lovely old Colt Navy pistol. I have a jeweller's lathe, a pendant drill and all manner of small metal-working instruments. Tiny machinery fascinates me.

Oh dear, this reads like a school essay. I imagine you correcting it with a red pencil! I'm sorry, Grace. Please bear with me. I would really enjoy to do this well.

Each morning and evening I walk through the park, to and from the office. It is a special joy to me. At all times of the year there is beauty.

I belong to a harriers club, swim twice a week and try to lead a well-balanced life. I suppose I do not have many close friends. In fact there are none. Perhaps you will become one, Grace. Alan McGill, our senior partner, is a decent sort. He has invited me to dinner once or twice.

Please keep writing. I miss my father; visiting him gave shape to my year. It is difficult to muster enthusiasm for visiting my brother. He and Sheila live in such a cultural desert.

I would very much like to visit you again if I am in Wellington. You have a beautiful home.

Yours sincerely,
Adam Friedmann

P.S. Enclosed is a photograph of the Navy Colt Pistol 1851. The engraving on the butt is mine. I copied it from a book.

Saturday May 7th

Dear Mildred,
I am so sorry to hear your health has deteriorated again. Christchurch is of course rather dank in the winter. I'm surprised you have not returned earlier. At least the wind keeps the air alive in Wellington. But now you must stay till this bout is over. Do not lose heart, Mildred, please. I would come down to visit, but feel this might be a sign that I approve of Judith's plan. I don't. You will be happier up here with your friends. I'm convinced of it.

It may well be that your illness is brought on by a form of depression; you miss your own surroundings and companions. Not to mention that wretched Cio-Cio. Your cat would be enough to keep me away for a lifetime but I know you're fond of the creature. I continue to feed him. He wanders, I'm afraid. The Wellford children entice him with food, and twice I have seen him sitting in their window looking smugly out at the rain. If you're not back soon, I fear you may lose his allegiance.

I've had my own little sick ward up here over the last two weeks. Sally Friedmann, Max's granddaughter, has been recuperating with me. I would not mention this, Mildred, but I know I can rely on your absolute discretion. Also your nursing experience may throw some light. I believe she has terminated a pregnancy. I hope this does not shock you too much.

To be honest, Mildred, I've been at my wits' end. The poor girl cries and cries. There have been times, I confess, when I could give her a good slap, though I do not believe in violence as you know.

Thank goodness she came to me. I hate to think of her going through this torment in her flat with all its comings and goings. There's no temperature or loss of appetite. She sleeps and sleeps. All the spark has gone out of her.

Well, I mustn't burden you with my problems. If Sally doesn't come right I will have to contact Martin and Sheila. But oh dear, you can imagine what their religious beliefs would make of this! From something Martin mentioned I suspect this may be Sally's second termination. I don't know, Mildred, I hope I am liberal minded, but I do find this casual attitude to life difficult, don't you?

Well, I mustn't be hard. It is clear Sally's attitude is not casual at the moment.

What do people in your area think of the political situation in Christchurch? I know you do not support Labour, but you may have heard some gossip. They seem to be tearing themselves apart. I am most disappointed.

Do keep up with the Vitamin C. In Christchurch there might almost be a case for putting it in the drinking water! All that smog and dank weather. I expect to hear that you are up and about in a week, and planning your return.

I do so miss you.

Please give my regards to Judith and the rest of the family.

Affectionately,
Grace

P.S. Would you like me to prune your roses? Your gardener simply cuts off the dead heads. Can you imagine!

Saturday May 21st

Dear Mildred,
It is a relief to know you are being so well looked after, though I wonder that Judith has time for you with all her social engagements. Everyone at the bowls club sends their love. If only you were in your own home we would all be round with soups and gossip! Are you aware just how many friends care for you in this area?

You will be delighted to know that your advice worked perfectly! I have to admit that when it comes to family or medical matters you leave me far behind. Sally is back on her perch and will return to Drama School next week. I was on the wrong track completely. Serves me right for listening to Les Comfrey's advice. I won't make that mistake again. To be honest, Mildred, I was beginning to fear an end like Gillian's, and was reluctant to leave Sally alone for a minute.

Well, there it is. I have certainly learnt a thing or two these last few days! I believed rest, quiet and good food would do the trick. But your prescription of a good dose of her own age group was just right. As soon as her flatmates poked their heads round the door with a bunch of flowers, she perked up. The flowers, by the way, looked suspiciously as if they had come from your garden!

Felix is her special friend. A nice enough lad, though not nearly of Sally's calibre. Evidently he has been home with his family. But surely he could call, if he's such a good friend. And why didn't Sally call him? Sally is very complicated, but it's not for me to interfere. Well, this Felix arrived and two others — and a transistor radio which has been blaring ever since. They sat on the bed and gossiped and ate me out of house and home and in no time Sally was pink cheeked and sitting up in bed.

It was all to do with money. I never understood the full story, but I gather Sally had been claiming some Social Security allowance to which she was not entitled, and was found out. She is not dishonest, Mildred, simply naïve. There was money to pay back, and a threat of legal action. As Felix pointed out, any of the others in the flat would have rung home and pleaded for a rescue cheque. Sally won't do that. Her parents would probably make leaving Drama School a condition. The poor girl was sick with anxiety — and shame — and fell into a depression. Once she explained to her friends they were full of advice. Debt, it seems, is a way of life with these students. I cannot approve.

Felix has been back every day for a week. I find I am warming to him. I've given the whole group a serious talk about budgeting. They hardly understand the word, Mildred, let alone how to draw up an annual plan. Fortunately I still have some of my old journals. It's all there in black and white — menus, entertainment allowance, a portion set aside for doctor's bills, and so on. I pointed out that they can eat like kings for a week, on a side of mutton, for the price of a single takeaway. They seem reluctant to take finances seriously, though. We live in a different era, I'm afraid.

Thank you, my dear, for your good sense. I was so worried. You know so much more than I do about the workings of young minds. This last week has been quite an education. However I have to admit the prospect of a peaceful, empty house is beginning to have a certain attraction. You must feel the same with all your grandchildren and great-grandchildren coming and going?

Have you come across Adam Friedmann? He is Max's other son — a lawyer in Christchurch. He's interested in cultured things, it seems. Perhaps he would be prepared to sponsor Sally through her studies. Or would it be meddling to suggest it? I would appreciate your advice.

Well my dear, I hope to see you soon. Cio-Cio is as well as can be expected.

Affectionately,
Grace

PROTEST

'Surely rugby wasn't your thing,' says Sally. She is looking again at the newspaper article.

SEVENTY-YEAR-OLD ARRESTED FOR CONVICTIONS she reads. Underneath, in smaller capitals:

> SPRINGBOK TOUR PROTESTER COMPLAINS ABOUT POLICE TREATMENT.
> Seventy-year-old Grace Brockie has little time for the legal system. 'When I asked to make a phone call,' she claims, 'they refused. At two in the morning, I was out on the street with no money, no transport. Is that the way to treat citizens who have not yet been proven guilty?'

The photograph shows a respectable, serious face, pointed chin, dark, bright eyes, grey hair pulled behind in a neat roll. It's certainly not the face one would connect with riots or police cells.

'Tell me about it,' says Sally.

Sally is researching for a drama assignment. Or that is the excuse. Grace suspects other reasons are behind the visit: the need for a square meal; personality clashes at the flat; further problems with money, perhaps. Grace never asks. She has learnt to keep quickly prepared food in the freezer, and always responds warmly to Sally's last-minute phone calls. Sometimes Sally is tense, jumpy and leaves without explanations. Tonight, though, the research project is perhaps genuine. Crosslegged at Grace's feet, one side of her face flushed from the fire, Sally seems relaxed and inquisitive. Grace loves these evenings.

'The 1981 tour,' says Grace, eager to be drawn, 'everyone knows about that.'

'But you, Grace, why you? You're not interested in rugby.'

Grace smiles. 'That's true. Mildred said the same thing at the time. But in 1981 there was madness in the air. An anger and an excitement that had little to do with games and a great deal to do with a divided society. The protest was a kind of safety valve. I believe those Saturday marches were as addictive, as bonding to us protesters, as the rugby matches were to sports enthusiasts. It was a heady time, Sally.'

'But breaking the law! You're so proper. Whatever made you run onto the airport?'

'Anger took over I suppose. With the government, with Air New Zealand for carrying an all-white team. With that wretched Muldoon. Then the gap in the fence appeared at the right time — or wrong. We simply ran through it.'

'Ran! You can't even run down the hall . . . '

'I'm not a complete cripple, Sally . . . '

'Well okay but . . . '

'And this was thirteen years ago, remember.'

'Even so . . . I just can't imagine you . . . '

'To be honest I couldn't have made it on my own. The others held my arms, hurried me forward. My short little legs hardly touched the ground. It must have looked ridiculous. I ran on air until my carriers couldn't take the weight any more. Then we all stopped. Oh, it was bitter out there, Sally. Wind, rain . . . the weather was definitely on the side of law and order.'

'Weren't you frightened?'

‘Yes. Nervous and excited, like a child on a forbidden escapade. Some protesters left. But most of us held our ground, not sure what to do. Alone on that vast expanse. The fervour drained away, then, like the rain off our coats. All that was left was an assorted bunch of wet citizens, standing in a puddle. I worried about dinner with Mildred, mainly.’

‘Why? Why dinner with Mildred?’

‘It was my birthday, Sally. Mildred is the only person who knows the date. She usually invites me over for something special. But down there at the police station, they wouldn’t let me use the phone.’

‘Hey, that’s not legal!’

‘No, it’s not. I knew my rights. One phone call is allowed. I told them my friend’s dinner would be spoiling. They simply didn’t care, Sally. It was most awkward. Mildred and I didn’t see eye to eye on the tour, you see.’

It was, in fact, the only time that Grace could remember when their friendship had frayed. Mildred came from a rugby family. A grandson was a provincial rep, perhaps even All Black material. Mildred’s family were outraged that liberals with no interest in the game should threaten their Saturday entertainment. No amount of rational argument on the evils of apartheid, the importance of taking a stand, of sending signals to the world would shake Mildred’s beliefs.

‘I hate apartheid too, Grace, don’t we all. But leave rugby out of it. You’re not a rugby person, Grace, and shouldn’t judge.’

Grace had been alarmed at her friend’s vehemence. The country was bitterly divided, that was obvious, but somehow she expected the long friendship with Mildred to override political or ideological difference. Grace would argue politics of the left all day, given the chance. Mildred, born into the

National Party, and unquestioning ever since, did not discuss politics. How you voted was between you and the ballot box in Mildred's view. However, in the months leading up to the protests, Grace thought she detected a fading in Mildred's true blue allegiance.

'You're right about one thing,' sighed Mildred. They were speaking of the Prime Minister, Muldoon. 'He's a nasty little man. Not at all like Holyoake. There was a gentleman. Mind you,' she added quickly, 'we need a strong leader.'

Grace, a zealous spark in her eye, plotted to capture Mildred for the left. But the Springbok Tour polarised people and Mildred's blue deepened again.

Grace found it difficult to disguise her burning indignation, her outrage with a spineless government. She wanted to rail against Mildred's stoic acceptance. But she learned to keep the fervour to herself; to slip away quietly to Saturday marches and weekday rallies. A silence developed though. There were fewer chats over coffee. Easy laughter as the sherry decanter tilted was a rarer pleasure. The birthday dinner was an olive branch; they both recognised it.

'Did you get out in time, Grace? For your birthday dinner?'

'Oh no. The police were beside themselves, I think. Cells were overflowing. Hundreds to fingerprint and photograph. They wanted to teach us a lesson and were frustrated by all the jollity. So they deliberately took their time.'

'Jollity. In a prison cell?'

'Well — yes! By then we were all veterans of many marches. There were songs.'

'But wasn't it frightening? Alone in a cell?'

'Alone? Goodness no. There must have been twenty or thirty in our cell, crammed in — nowhere to sit. People started up conversations, discovered they had common friends or relations . . . You couldn't hear yourself think!'

'Sounds romantic. You meet any nice men, Grace?'

'No no no, none of that! They separated the sexes right on the airport. Husbands and wives had no idea where their partners were.'

'Hey, this is real drama! Families ripped apart!'

'Well, that was certainly the worst part. After the airport, they shut us up in the dog pound, I think it was.'

'You're making it up . . . '

'No I'm not, Sally. It was a yard, out in the rain, with wire-mesh fences. Men in one cage, women in the other. Then they bundled us into windowless vans. We had no idea where we were going. The cells were quite cosy after that.'

'Did you know anyone?'

'Not really. They were friendly, though, the women. Offered me a place on the one bench. The men were somewhere near — they joined in when we started singing. I remember one woman . . . '

Grace sees again the large cheerful woman gripping the bars of their cell door, looking out. In a small voice she started up 'Drink to Me Only'. The song grew and blossomed down the corridor, taken up by cell after cell until the sound, echoing off the brick, swelled into a rich choir. When the voices died, she listened for a moment longer, and then nodded, pleased.

'That was Michael's tenor,' she said, 'He's down there somewhere.' And she began her roll call. 'Michael? Is that you?'

'Yes, love.' A hand waved through bars.

'Andrew?'

'Yes, Mum, in with Dad.'

'Jonathan?'

'Yes, Mum.'

And so on, five children, till she had them all placed. Then she turned to her cellmates proudly. 'Beat that,' she said. 'All good kids, eh?'

Grace shakes her head. 'She was proud of them, you see. Proud that her children were arrested.'

'Her whole family in the cells?'

'The whole family, Sally.'

'Boy, you'd never get teenagers doing that sort of thing as a family now.'

'Yes. You may be right. It was a strange time.'

'Go on. How'd you get out? A mass escape?'

'Well, it stopped being fun, after a while. We were taken out one by one. Stood against a dirty white wall with heights marked on it. Photographed with a sign giving us a number. Then hurried back to the cell. Others were outraged at the indignity. But Mildred and the spoiling dinner were in the end more important to me. Just that once I could have missed a march, or marched in a safer place. I felt ashamed, Sally.'

'But you made a mark, helped change a cruel system! Didn't you say that photograph of the protesting seventy-year-old went round the world? Aren't you proud?'

'Perhaps a little. People wrote to me. Most of it was simple hate-mail. Not important. One letter really shook me, though. The woman was elderly. She had been flying in to visit a daughter. It was her first plane trip and she was both nervous and excited. Then her plane's descent was aborted because there were protesters on the runway. Round and round it circled till the police had cleared us all away. She feared the plane would run out of fuel; she felt she was about to die. She wrote that because of my actions she would never fly again.'

'The pilot would never risk the passengers' lives.'

'No, but the woman feared it. Was running onto the airport worth that, I wonder?'

'Yes!' says Sally with conviction. She unfolds her neat legs and paces the room. She tries out a pose or two.

'*Amandla*!' she cries, waving a protest banner. 'We shall overco-o-ome,' she sings. 'No, Grace, your protest was right and just. I would run onto the airport for my convictions!'

'Good,' says Grace, and means it. 'But perhaps you'll have to run for me next time.'

'Nonsense. We'll pop you in a wheelchair and you can scream slogans while I push. Boadicea strikes again!'

They both laugh out loud. Thank you, Max, for this wonderful child, thinks Grace.

'And did the dinner spoil?' asks Sally. 'Did Mildred forgive you?'

'Oh Mildred,' says Grace smiling. 'Mildred was there to meet me when I came out of prison.'

One by one, according to no discernible hierarchy, they had been released. At half past two in the morning Grace climbed the steps from the cells and walked into cold, wet Waring Taylor Street. Money and car were far away at the airport. Grace did not know how to get home, how to reach her car.

'Grace, you look chilled to the bone,' said Mildred. 'Get in quick, there's a blanket and a thermos on the back seat.'

Relief and delight warmed Grace as much as Mildred's generously laced coffee.

'But how did you know? I tried to phone, Mildred, but those police . . . '

'Don't tell me about the police,' said Mildred through tight lips. 'Yes, I'll have another drop, we need it at this time of night. I saw you on telly, you see. It gave me a shock, Grace. Surely that was unwise, with a birthday dinner in the making!'

'I'm sorry,' said Grace humbly.

'You did look lonely out there on the tarmac. Not that I condone it, of course.'

'No.'

'So I rang the police station and told them it was your birthday. I explained it was salmon mornay and would spoil . . . '

'Salmon mornay? Oh dear, Mildred . . . '

'And lemon meringue pie, your favourite. The policewoman was barely civil, Grace. It cut no ice at all.'

Mildred's indignation, and perhaps exhaustion, had moved Grace to tears. 'Well, no harm,' said Mildred, smiling at her friend. 'It was on the six o'clock news I saw you. There was time to save the salmon. We'll have it tomorrow.'

Sally looks up from her writing. 'Would you mind if I used this? We have to do a monologue. I could fight your cause all over again. Sally Friedmann stars as famous protester Grace Brockie!'

Grace smiles, flattered. 'Well. You really think people would be interested?' She adds, after a while, 'And will your parents come to the performance?'

Sally's lively face clouds. 'No. No, of course not. Acting is the devil's work, don't you know.'

I have another battle ahead of me, thinks Grace.

18th July

Dear Adam,
Thank you for your interesting letter. Certainly I was wrong ever to suggest that your life was devoid of activity! I felt quite tired reading about it.

I'm sorry if I give you the impression that I'm lying in wait to pounce on your letters and assess them. Of course that is not so. But when you have taught English for years it's hard to escape the correcting habit. Sometimes when reading the paper, I find my hand has picked up a pen and I am mechanically inserting full-stops or erasing apostrophes, without registering at all what I am doing. Just as well there is no one watching me. They would think it was time for the rest home! At any rate you write beautifully correct English.

Now, Adam. It is good to hear you have so many worthwhile activities, but I must say I've been distressed to read about your guns. Manual activity can be a wonderful companion, but surely there is a better vehicle for your craft skills. We read so many times of guns getting into the wrong hands. Do you have them locked away?

You do not sound like an aggressive man. Why choose such weapons of destruction for a hobby? I am surprised at you.

Oh dear. The schoolteacher again! I can hear Max laughing. He would be arguing with me by now if he were here. But I would argue back, never fear. I feel very strongly about guns.

Have you thought of jewellery-making? Your

beautiful engraving could be put to more peaceful use. I tell you what. I will order a piece from you. A little brooch with the same motif as the one on the butt of the Colt Navy pistol. This is a commercial proposition, Adam. Charge me properly for your labour. Well, perhaps not legal rates, I'm not a millionaire.

I would enjoy having something made by you.

Adam, you sound rather depressed. Max often told me I concentrated too much on activity and not enough on cultivating friends. At the moment, with Mildred in Christchurch, I know I'm retreating, and have to speak to myself severely. Perhaps you need to work hard at friendship too. You need good friends, Adam, who share your interests.

Perhaps you might start with your niece, Sally. She can't appeal to her parents for assistance of any sort, let alone financial. I don't wish to meddle, and Mildred has advised against it, but you may think of some little way to help her. I'll just leave the thought with you.

Tertiary education should be free. I am most disappointed that the Labour Party has not stood behind its principles. You will no doubt disagree. As a lawyer, I expect you vote National. What is happening to Christchurch politics? I always thought of your city as sensible, if not downright stolid, but now it seems the Labour stronghold is breaking apart. What is Anderton up to? I would welcome your views.

At this time of year I can identify strongly with pagan beliefs. No wonder they held festivals to celebrate the rebirth of life. I long for spring. We have had a whole week of gales and squally rain. Everywhere there is black cold. The sun can barely manage to bring daylight, and soon gives up the struggle.

Well, Adam, don't take any notice of my grumpiness. I do like to be able to get outside. A few fine, crisp winter days and I'll be singing like a bird again!

Thank you for writing. It cheered up the week. But do think again about the guns. I'm sure the museum would be pleased to accept your collection.

Yours sincerely,
Grace

P.S. Are you keeping up with Vitamin C? Max was not good at remembering. Citrus and kiwifruit are the best sources. G

Friday 22nd July

Dear Grace,
Thank you for your kind letter. I am enjoying our correspondence more than I can say. You are right, I should have more friends, be more social, but somehow I lose heart. People don't find me much fun, I'm afraid.

Grace, I hesitate to bring up this matter. The last thing I want to do is drive you away, or shock you. I don't know who else to turn to. Also you have been a teacher and may be able to advise me.

A rather terrible thing happened last week.

I believe my last letter mentioned that I was to visit Christ's College. The boys are studying different professions and our firm was approached to supply a legal expert. I volunteered mainly because I felt it would be a challenge; my speaking skills would be enlarged. Mr McGill, our senior partner, has often suggested that I need to be more outgoing.

On the day in question I arrived in good time. The headmaster showed me to the classroom. The boys were working quietly at their desks. I sat at the rear of the room in an empty desk and watched. I could see the work of the boy next to me, and was fascinated by his writing. I trust it was fiction. The boy had a bizarre imagination. Before I went to the front I complimented him on his work.

During my little talk, which I believe went quite well, we invented some legal problems and the boys, acting as clients, came to me for a legal opinion. The young lad at the back was particularly adept at holding a role, and we had quite a spirited exchange over buying a business.

That was that, really. I felt modestly pleased with the event. I invited those who were interested, to visit our law firm later in the week to view the real thing. This had been cleared with their teacher and Mr McGill in advance. I believe in following the proper channels.

As I left, I had a word with the bright little writer. He had a real understanding of legal issues, and I urged him to join the trip to the office. Perhaps I was too friendly, but I cannot really think so.

On the way out the teacher was kind enough to suggest that the visit had been educationally successful.

I apologise, Grace, if this account seems long winded, but I wish you to understand the sequence of events clearly.

A few days later a handful of boys visited the office. Jeremy Atkinson was one of them: the writer from the back of the room. Perhaps I paid more attention to him than the other boys. Certainly he came into my office and tried out my swivel chair. He seemed outgoing and I enjoyed his company. I gave him a promotional ball-point which we present to clients. In retrospect this was perhaps unwise. I should have treated all the boys equally.

They all left and the office returned to normal.

The shock came two days later. The headmaster, Mr Willard-Smith, rang and asked me to call into his office. I expected this would be some sort of official thanks. How wrong I was! It appeared that young Jeremy had laid a complaint against me. You can imagine how devastated I was. Nothing like this has happened to me before. Why should the boy make such allegations? I can hardly bear to write what he claimed. I became quite flustered, I'm afraid, which perhaps did not help my case.

Fortunately the head is a decent sort. He told me from the beginning that young Jeremy has a history of making this sort of allegation; that he has had a disturbed background; but that it was his duty to follow up any story, no matter how improbable it seemed. All this was reassuring but the question remained — why did the lad choose me? I could tell that Mr Willard-Smith was asking himself the same question. It was dreadfully embarrassing.

I described my encounters with Jeremy carefully. My memory is excellent. The head remarked on the detail. Immediately I worried that my story was too accurate; that a hazy recall might seem more credible. It is damnable to be in such a situation. I do remember that as Jeremy left my office I put my hand on his shoulder, and gave him a — pat, I suppose you would call it. Perhaps I did it awkwardly. I wanted to be friendly and natural. Alan McGill would have carried it off with ease no doubt. I wonder whether my very hesitation rang some bell in Jeremy's nasty mind. I cannot feel sorry for him, the wretched boy.

You have been a teacher, Grace. Can you imagine

why a boy would make up these accusations?

It is a great blow. The one occasion when I tried to be more sociable; to come out of my shell as it were, I am landed in this mess. I cannot help but feel bitter.

Mr Willard-Smith has had to ask for corroborating statements from my colleagues and from the other boys. If the boy has such a reputation, why could the matter have not been kept private? I must have been in some way under suspicion.

Finally the allegation was dropped, thank goodness, but the damage is done anyway. Though the other partners have been supportive, a seed has been sown in their minds. Could I have touched the boy improperly, they wonder. No smoke without a fire, they suggest when I am out of the room. I begin to doubt myself.

Please advise me.

I have little heart for other matters. Another time I will argue the case for guns. They are beautiful things. A duelling pistol by Boutet, for example is a work of art equal to the finest jewellery. Almost all my collection are antiques, collected for their style or historical interest. They give me great pleasure. I do not intend to doubt my abilities in this area too.

Forgive my depression. This has been a difficult week. I am glad to be able to write to you. You will understand my predicament I am sure.

I would be honoured to make you a little brooch. The catch may be beyond my capabilities, but there are good instruction manuals in the library. When is your birthday? That would give me a deadline towards which I could work.

I, too, long for spring.

Yours faithfully,
Adam Friedmann

Sunday 31st July

Dear Grace,
Why don't you write? My life has turned into a nightmare. I suppose you have read about Jeremy Atkinson. I did not harm the boy. Surely you cannot imagine that I did?

The police have been all over the house. They clearly suspect me.

What should I do? You are my only friend. Please, please do not desert me.

Yours faithfully,
Adam

Sunday 7th August

Dear Grace,
Yesterday I hoped for a letter from you so much that I found an excuse to wait in the foyer at mail time. Nothing came. I can only suppose you have been frightened away by the terrible events.

I apologise for my outburst a few days ago. It does no one any good to panic, but this is all so bizarre. I keep thinking that the darkness will clear. It goes on. The terrible thing is not knowing. Do the police really suspect me? Surely they can see I am harmless. Yet I have been questioned twice and cautioned not to leave town! They must see I am not violent. I wonder whether they are pursuing my story with such vigour in order to flush out some other offender. They must have a more likely suspect. Don't you think?

It is important to stay calm. I must order events clearly in my mind. Sooner or later some piece of evidence will exonerate me, but meantime I must be absolutely certain of my details. The police are methodical themselves and will surely respect an orderly account.

The trouble, Grace, is that circumstantially things look bad for me. First there was the incident at Christ's College. I wish to God that I had never set a foot inside the place. Jeremy Atkinson's accusation left a stain, even though I was exonerated.

But there is worse. I hesitate to tell you this; I want so desperately for you to believe me, but I must be utterly truthful if I am to survive. I believe you are the sort of person to recognise the truth if it is laid out clearly before you.

I have told the police all this.

On the night Jeremy was attacked I met him in Hagley Park. It would be more accurate to say he met me. I was walking home as usual, at 5.15. It was almost dark. He called my name — 'Mr Friedmann!' I turned and there was Jeremy, self-assured and smiling, as if nothing had happened. You can imagine I was not at all pleased to see him. I turned away, but he followed, chatting to me behind my back. I believe, Grace, the boy is not quite normal. I don't mean retarded; he was clearly bright, but his chatter was too cheerful, brittle. There was an edge of something under the babble. Fear perhaps? Or loneliness? He didn't seem quite in control of his words. In other circumstances I might have felt sorry for him. As darkness fell it would be responsible to make sure he got home safely. But naturally I felt it was important at all costs to avoid contact with him. The damnable thing was, Jeremy seemed set on following me home.

Finally I turned to face him. He stopped.

'Jeremy, go home,' I said.

It was like speaking to a dog, Grace. He just smiled and came closer. I think he would have taken my hand had I not stepped back. I became alarmed.

'You have done me a great harm, Jeremy,' I said, 'You must go away before you do more. Now go. Quickly!'

I spoke quite sharply, hoping to shake him into

some action. To be honest I was fearful someone would walk past — the exchange took place on a public path through the park. This encounter would look far less innocent than Jeremy's visit to the office.

I now know that someone did see and hear us.

Suddenly Jeremy changed. He is a tall lad for fourteen and, as I said, rather confident. But in a moment his face became that of an angry child. He shouted back at me.

'Go away yourself! Get out! Slimy old creep!'

He ran at me and pushed hard. My foot caught on the edge of the pathway and I fell heavily onto the muddy grass. By the time I had righted myself he was running away.

You can imagine it was with some relief that I continued home and shut the door on the whole incident. Parents who let their children wander alone at night should be prosecuted.

Next morning I heard on the news that a boy had been assaulted and left unconscious in the park. The name was not released, but I had a terrible premonition that it was Jeremy. I could not face work, and stayed home, waiting to hear the worst. By midday the name was released. All afternoon I prevaricated over going to the police. I should go, and yet my evidence seemed so incriminating. And I could tell them nothing that would help find the assailant. Or so I reasoned.

The police came to me first. It threw the worst possible light on my actions. They had already uncovered the Christ's incident, and someone had reported seeing a man, whose description fitted me, struggling with Jeremy in Hagley Park. Now my account sounded like an unconvincing attempt to clear myself. Why wasn't I at work, they wanted to know. Why were my clothes muddy?

The minute they found my gun collection I believe the detective decided the case was closed. It seems the attacker had carried a gun.

It is all circumstantial. They have not charged me. But I feel that they have stopped looking for anyone else.

Alan McGill and the others at the office have been very decent. They know all about innocent until proved guilty. They would rather I took a holiday, but I would go mad, Grace.

At least the papers have not got hold of me. I could not cope with that. The police have been searching the park endlessly, especially near my flat. Some of the residents saw the police come to me; I suppose they have been questioned about my movements. Surely one of them saw me arrive home before the boy was attacked?

No one talks to me. The police are silent.

Please believe me, Grace. I am not violent.

Yours faithfully,
Adam Friedmann

10th August

Dear Adam,
Please excuse my delay in writing. Your letters have been a great shock to me. I have been trying to decide whether to respond.

Have you told the police about our letters? I would rather you didn't. It would be difficult for me if police came questioning.

You must see, Adam that I don't know you very well. I'm an elderly woman, living on my own, and should not take risks. It would seem, at present, that you are at least a risk. Anyone, Mildred especially if she knew, would advise me to break off all communication with you immediately.

On the other hand you are Max's son. You cared for him when he was ill. I have reread all your letters carefully and they have the ring of truth about them. I have decided to keep writing for the present. Perhaps I can help you. But please will you keep our correspondence private?

It is clear you are in a difficult position. Possibly the only thing you can do is to wait. I imagine you have legal advice from your colleagues. Perhaps it would be useful to consider the boy more carefully. I believe you are being hard on him. Poor lad. Rather than lay out facts and events, turn your mind to whys and wherefores.

Why was Jeremy following you? What did he really want to communicate to you? Did he give some clue as to where he was going next? The papers haven't mentioned that he's disturbed. Only that he comes from a rather respected family, that his mother is well known in Christchurch society and that the family is devastated.

Make sure, Adam, that you are being honest with yourself. And me.

I do not believe you attacked the boy. But perhaps there's more to be told? The police need to be watched with care. Many years ago I was arrested. This will surprise you, no doubt. It was during the Springbok Tour demonstrations of 1981. I was only seventy then, and felt very strongly about apartheid. Most Saturdays I joined a march and on one, at Wellington airport, I was arrested. The charge was trespass on a security area — a criminal offence it seemed, serious enough to warrant a jury trial.

Well, it was all very traumatic at the time. A group of us were herded into police vans and held most of the night in the cells, without any way of communicating with the outside world.

Well what I am getting round to telling you, Adam, is that during the trial, the police lied. I was deeply shocked at the time and have not quite trusted police evidence since. Evidently when one is caught trespassing the arresting officer is bound utter a warning: 'You are trespassing and I advise you to disperse immediately or you will be arrested'. Something like that.

No one warned us. On that I'm quite clear, and so were the rest of our group. Yet one policeman swore in court that he had given the warning, and two others corroborated his evidence! If they saw fit to lie on such an unimportant issue, what else might they get up to when there is a great deal of public pressure?

So my advice, as a convicted criminal, is to be straight with the police but keep your distance. Make a written account of all your interviews with them, and ask the policeman to sign a copy. Don't leave all the writing to them.

I am a great believer, as you know, in the power of the written word.

It is unkind, I suppose, to attack a man when he's down, but Adam, everything I've said about guns is surely borne out now. You gun collection has marked you in police eyes.

What if someone broke into your flat, stole a gun and then killed with it? You would feel responsible. Rightly responsible. Guilt would definitely be appropriate then. No, Adam, get rid of your collection.

Well, the crisp sunny days are putting heart into us all. This is Wellington at its best. My stylosa are flowering wonderfully. I pick a bowlful every other day.

Take heart yourself. As you say, surely some other evidence will soon turn the police away from you.

All the best.

Kind regards,
Grace

P.S. Today a clear memory of you as a child came to me. I was sitting in your sunny kitchen, with Ilona, your mother. You were four perhaps. Gillie was not conceived. I was newly married — a thirty-five-year-old schoolteacher with no knowledge of family life. You were down on your haunches under the window, in a shaft of sunlight, singing to a beetle. I was entranced. On and on you sang — a long rambling saga about the beetle's family connections and home life. Neither your mother nor I dared make a sound for fear we broke the spell. You were utterly happy, I think. Goodness knows why I remember it, but I do. From that moment I longed for a child of my own.

Do not be downhearted.

My birthday is September 24th. I am a Libran. What about you?

Wednesday 17th August

Dear Grace,
Thank you so much for writing. You cannot believe what it means to me to have a friend.

Word is getting round. The papers have not mentioned my name, but have hinted that a Christchurch lawyer is under suspicion, and that the police expect to make an arrest soon.

In my block of flats the atmosphere is deadly. People look the other way when I go past. They think I did it, Grace. How can they? None of them are close friends, but we have had a word now and then. If they stopped to think, they would surely know I am incapable of violence.

Mrs Aylesford in Number 2A was collecting her mail at the same time as me yesterday. I said good morning and tried to smile.

'Go away,' she whispered, 'go away.' And stood there, white faced.

I went away. How is it possible? I now frighten old ladies.

At work, the partners have asked again if I will take leave. This time the suggestion was firmer. Yet the police do not wish me to leave town. So here I am on my own, with long, waiting days. I still swim and run, but could not face the Friends of the Opera evening last week.

I am working on your brooch.

Did you read in the papers that they have found a gun in the park? It was evidently an old Webley

Green revolver, not part of my collection at all. The only Webley I possess is a single-action Royal Irish Constabulary revolver. Quite a different weapon, and still in my gun case. Yes, it is securely locked, Grace. At first the news of the discovery pleased me, as I had supplied all my records to the police. My journal of acquisitions is meticulously kept, and there is no mention of a Webley Green. However the police took a different view. The fact that this is an old gun, convinced them that it must have been part of my collection, and that I had somehow cleverly concealed my ownership. It is ludicrous.

You ask me to consider the whys of the case rather than the facts. I have tried to do so honestly, Grace.

Why did Jeremy accuse me of molesting him?

I may have been attracted to him. Yes I suppose I was. People assume a single male of my age is homosexual. Especially if one is quiet and a little fussy. In my case it is true, though what does that prove? I have had only two relationships with men, many years ago. Perhaps Jeremy felt something from me. He is an attractive lad. But he must have experienced more overt sexual advances in the past, in order to make up the story. I am a shy man, Grace.

Jeremy has evidently not identified me as his attacker, though he suggests it was someone of my build. So the police say. Are they telling me the truth?

There is much about Jeremy that we are not hearing. His mother moves in society here. I have seen her on display at opera functions. She has no lack of boyfriends, many of them influential. From the little I know of the lad I would say there is a cover-up in play. His mother is pulling strings. Jeremy is certainly not the tragic innocent portrayed in the media. Surely a police investigation into his background and acquaintances might be fruitful? Yet they seem to have settled on me — the easy, obvious target; the outwardly quiet, inwardly festering paedophile.

I am not, Grace. I am not. You have urged me to be positive. God knows it is difficult with the whole world suspecting me.

Some citizen has reported seeing me 'hanging round' the playing fields, 'ogling' young boys. 'Hanging round'! 'Ogling'! A policeman read me the report. How words distort.

In the summer, I do indeed enjoy watching them play. It gives me pleasure. Is it a sexual pleasure, this arrogant policeman asked. I do not know! I do not want to know. To me it was a simple, harmless pleasure. Now it is tainted forever.

I have been completely honest with you. More honest than you would wish, perhaps.

The process has been helpful to me. Thank you for that. My depression has shifted somewhat towards anger. If they arrest me I will fight this with all my intelligence.

The waiting is difficult though. My collection of opera CDs is a comfort.

Martin and Sheila have heard rumours. News travels round this country on the wind it seems. They suggest that I do not have any further contact with them in the meantime. They have their children to think of! What nonsense: they are thinking of themselves. Tom and Sally are far more accepting.

I am happy to stay away.

You are another matter. I long for a quiet dinner with you in some civilised restaurant. It is a pleasure that I hold in front of me. Bless you.

Yours in friendship,
Adam

24th August

Dear Adam,
Your letter was both interesting and positive. I am impressed with your stamina. What a terrible time you are having.

Do, please, make sure you eat sensibly; you will need all your strength. Have you tried yeast flakes? They are surprisingly delicious and a good tonic. I believe deeply in the power good health brings us all. If you have spare time, Adam, try cooking new dishes. I will enclose my recipe for tuna fish pie. Max was fond of it.

I have written to my friend Mildred about your case. You will remember Mildred Catherwood from across the park? She is staying in Christchurch with her daughter. Naturally I did not bring up the matter; I am not one to spread gossip. However Mildred had heard you were implicated. Her daughter Judith is rather a scandalmonger, I'm afraid — good at heart, perhaps, but always out for a good time.

Evidently Judith's lawyer works at your firm and he told her. You are right, Adam, how gossip spreads. Judith would be the last person to whom one would entrust confidential information. Quite possibly she has been responsible, single handedly, for spreading your name throughout New Zealand. I wouldn't say that to Mildred, of course.

As far as Judith is concerned you are convicted and sentenced. I soon put Mildred right on that one!

At first Mildred was adamant that I should break all communication with you. Our correspondence might incriminate me, Mildred fears, especially given my criminal record. Mildred is rather cautious over the law.

I felt it best to lay all the facts before her. Forgive me if my action upsets you, Adam. This was a breach of confidence, I know, but you need friends. And now you have a new one. Mildred has become convinced, as I am, that you are innocent. She may run on at times, but Mildred is no fool.

We both feel you need more support in Christchurch. Surely there are people — at work or one of your many clubs — who would act as character witnesses for you? I would advise against the gun club. What about your opera friends? Some of them must be influential.

I'm afraid that your solitary nature mitigates against you. Mildred feels that you may be encouraging accusations by withdrawing into yourself. Well, that is easier said than done, I know. I am not the most outgoing person myself.

But you must make an effort, Adam!

Mildred will do what she can too. She has a nephew in the police force down there; someone influential I believe.

Perhaps she can cause a little change in attitude. Mildred is very sociable and unshakably respectable. Her family is well known in Christchurch, coming as they did on the first four ships. She would be a good ambassador for you.

Well, we mustn't get our hopes too high. At least the

papers have dropped the story. It's all the in-vitro issue now.

What is your opinion? I can sympathise with single women and old women wanting babies, but really you must draw the line somewhere. There are far too many people in the world as it is.

I'm a great believer, Adam, and you will probably agree with me here, in the value of single people, who are unencumbered with children. Society needs them. I wonder what Max would have thought?

Well, Adam, have patience. Surely the truth will surface in the end. You may wish to ring Mildred. Her daughter's number is under J. E. Trevelyan in Fendalton. Mildred says it is not far from Hagley Park.

Take heart; keep thinking positively.

Your friend,
Grace

P.S. Enclosed my recipe for tuna fish pie. You may add sour cream if you're feeling adventurous. G

Saturday 27th August

Dear Grace,

Thank you for the tuna recipe. I *was* feeling adventurous and so substituted smoked salmon pieces for the tuna *and* added sour cream! Do not think that you are the only one with a culinary interest. Thai cooking is my particular area. I am quite proud of my spicy beef on jasmine rice. Also I bake bread in the weekends. The smell of hot yeasty bread is such a friendly aroma, don't you think? The other residents often joke about the 'lovely Saturday smell at Flat 4A'. Or they used to. I baked again this morning for the first time in weeks.

This is a wonderful winter day. I am sitting on my balcony looking out to the Alps. They are snow covered into the distance.

You letter gave me such heart. And I have seen Mildred, just this morning! As soon as the bread was out and cooling, I went for a walk on the park. You see, Grace, I am trying to keep up a normal life. I saw two women walking ahead. One, I am sure, was Mrs Catherwood — Mildred. I remember her from years back — but was not sure she would want to see me. I followed like some amateur detective. There she was, unmistakably the same. She is rather a regal person, don't you think, a little like the Queen Mother.

The other was, I suppose, her daughter. Her clothes were out of a fashion magazine. All good wool in earthy colours, falling just so. She is tall and slim and walks like a model. Mildred looked much more comfortable to me. I longed to approach her and introduce myself.

She would be a good friend I could see. You are lucky to have her.

Now I am back at my flat. I know it sounds childish, but seeing Mildred so solidly placing her feet one in front of the other gave a feeling of the cavalry arriving! I am foolish to hope. But as you say it is important to be positive. I will ring Mildred this afternoon.

My bread has turned out well. This batch has sunflower seeds and chopped walnuts in a rye and white mix of flour.

You may be surprised to know that I do not agree with you over artificial insemination. If a single person wishes so strongly to have a child, are not the chances good that she will become a satisfactory mother? So many people are unsuitable parents, or unwilling parents. We come across many in the legal profession. Jeremy Atkinson's mother is possibly a case in point. I believe, Grace, that in-vitro fertilisation may well push the scale towards better parenting. Goodness knows solo parents are becoming the norm now anyway.

The first flower spikes are appearing on my Cape primroses. I will have a spectacular display.

Later —

Perhaps I will not be around to see my flowers. The police came just after lunch and took me down to the station. They have not arrested me but will shortly, I believe. I don't know what to say, Grace. This world has turned into an alien planet.

They say they have fresh evidence linking me to

Jeremy. They believe nothing I say. I believe they are trying to frighten me. They certainly succeeded. With my heart pounding, I have just tried to ring Mildred as you suggested. A woman answered. Judith I expect. I asked for Mrs Catherwood. When my name was requested, I gave it; a natural reflex, though unwise in the circumstances.

She put down the receiver. Simply replaced it quietly without a word. I fear I am done for, Grace.

Your friend,
Adam

Tuesday 30th August

Dear Grace,
I am still here.

Yesterday I lunched with Mildred at the Dux de Lux. Her phone call came just after I had posted a letter to you. What an exceedingly pleasant woman! So polite and considerate. I must say she is looking frail, though she insisted her health is improving. We sat in a private corner, and she treated me as if there were no cloud hanging over me at all.

She chose fish pie and I had the soup, which is always good there.

Mildred questioned me quite carefully. I had to hide my smile, Grace. Mildred turns the most serious matter into a small domestic problem. As far as she is concerned it is only a matter of someone making the right connections. I fear there is more to it than that, and that the police are manufacturing evidence.

A spring sun was out yesterday. Narcissi were flowering outside the window. It felt so comfortable and safe, talking to Mildred I could have stayed there all day. She chatted on about this and that. I gather staying with her daughter is a bit of a trial. The son is still at home, and the house feels full of large people all wanting to use the bathroom at the same time! I gather she has a hard decision to make; whether to shift down here permanently or not. I know I would put a friend like you before family!

Mildred talked about you, too, Grace. I suppose

I was rather pumping her. She implies that you are lonely. I cannot quite imagine that anyone with a friend as chatty as Mildred could be lonely. However, I had not realised that you had so little connection with family. That is not easy when you are older, I am sure. If this episode of my life ever settles down, I would like to visit you regularly. Or would you care to visit me when Mildred is down with her family?

How tempting to dream. At the moment the nightmare continues. I jump at every sound, expecting an arresting officer.

Your suggestion of arranging character witnesses was a good one. I have spoken to the secretary of the Friends of the Opera. He is a decent sort. He had heard rumours about me but could not believe them true, and was quite shocked to hear how far the police investigation has gone. He talked of Jeremy Atkinson's background. Evidently the boy has some wild friends, mostly sons of wealthy families. Opera gossip has it that they got up to some rather questionable behaviour. John thinks it far more likely that one of this group was involved in the attack. He volunteered to speak to a friend of his who has influence.

This news is both hopeful and demoralising. Surely, if I am innocent, it will not come to an arrest. And yet, if people are influential enough to whitewash the boy's reputation, perhaps they can also bend the true course of justice.

I will post this now. Thank you so much for your

help and encouragement. Whatever happens I will try to keep contact if you wish it.

Your friend,
Adam

P.S. Enclosed is the brooch. Happy early birthday!

Wednesday 31st August

Dear Grace,
Well my dear, the weather has taken a turn for the worse, winter is back with a vengeance. This morning it was hailstones as big as my anti-inflammatory pills, that's not a word of exaggeration! I do hope they have not reached Wellington, my primulas would be ruined.

I've done what I can about Adam. A nice quiet man. Rather a stick of limp celery, don't you think? I'm sure he has done no wrong, he wouldn't say boo to a goose!

On Tuesday I invited Hamish, my nephew, to lunch. Judith made us a nice asparagus quiche. She uses dry vermouth in the egg mixture, it is worth trying. We all had a good chat. Hamish is very attractive, a real charmer and bright as a button, Judith was very attentive!

Over coffee I steered the conversation round to the attack. I mentioned that I'd heard Jeremy Atkinson had a reputation for hanging around with a rough group. Hamish pricked up his ears. Young gangs are his territory, I gather, he is in youth work. Well, suddenly some penny dropped, you could see it all over his face, he's wonderfully open.

'Cat-skin!' he said. 'I knew his photo was familiar!' And he jumped up and kissed me, just like that.

Honestly, Grace it makes you wonder. It turns out the photo of Jeremy being circulated is a school one, all brushed hair and smart uniform looking like butter wouldn't melt. His mother evidently kept the dark side of the boy to herself. Hamish knew Jeremy, by his nickname 'Cat-skin' — from Atkinson, I suppose — a strange lad, who dresses outlandishly and stays out till all hours in the park. Hamish had never made the connection to the assaulted boy.

Well, suddenly my nephew was all efficiency, up on his feet and no more chat. Something was going on in his mind, that was clear, but he wasn't saying a word. We were dying to know, but you have to admire discretion when you see it, it's rare enough when all is said and done.

I won't ring Adam just yet. It would be unkind to raise his hopes, and perhaps it will all come to nothing, but I will be most disappointed if the police can't follow up a few simple leads. They tell the public to co-operate and we do our best, but are they up to their side of it, Grace? I would love to have a good chat with you about it all, over a glass of sherry. Judith only has G and T, a depressing drink.

Judith's house is like a railway station these days. My grandson has shifts at all hours. He bangs around in the kitchen looking for food in the middle of the night, and barges into the toilet never mind knocking.

'At least get a lock, Judith,' I said. 'That boy is a menace to life and limb,' but I don't know, she is so busy with her clubs and morning teas, locks get missed in the rush.

Oh dear, Grace, I don't know what to do. They have built a granny flat you see. It's almost finished. They seem to assume I will stay on. You say be firm, but it is not so easy for me.

Tomorrow Judith is taking me out to Sumner, it's her bridge day. Her daughter will take me and the little ones for a walk on the beach. I'm exhausted thinking about it, they gallop around like puppies, there is no way I can keep up. I would rather play a few quiet heads with the bowls club I can tell you!

Oh dear what a screed, I must fly. Let's hope for better weather tomorrow.

All the best, dear, you will be finding it quiet without your chatterbox of a neighbour!

Please give my regards to the bowls club, they will be breaking for the summer soon.

Affectionately,
Mildred

Extract from *The Christchurch Star*, Thursday 1 September 1994:

YOUTHS CHARGED IN ATKINSON ASSAULT

In a shock move today, police apprehended two youths in connection with the assault of Jeremy Atkinson. The youths' names have not been released, but it is understood that both come from well-known Christchurch families.

In a statement, the police said that they had conducted exhaustive inquiries over the past month, which had led to this morning's action. As both youths are under age they will not be charged in the district court. The motive for the attack is not known at this stage.

The *Star* understands that the apprehended boys belong to a gang headed by Atkinson, and that this gang has been involved in minor drug abuse and disturbances of the peace.

Atkinson's mother was not available for comment.

Detective Inspector Potts paid a tribute to the police team which has worked 'round the clock' on this case for the last month.

'In the end it is hard slog and attention to detail that brings in the results,' he said. 'My men have done a tremendous job.'

Friday 2nd September

Dear Grace,
I am so overcome I do not know what to say.

The police crow on about their arrest. Let them.

As far as I'm concerned you and Mildred are the ones to receive medals. Your good advice and sound common sense have achieved far more than all their investigations.

Thank you. Without your kindness and belief in me I would not have survived, I think.

What else can I say?

I have presented my gun collection to the museum. They can dispose of it as they wish.

You are about to receive a bunch of the best spring flowers New Zealand can grow.

Thank you,
Adam

Sunday 4th September

Dear Adam,
The brooch is exquisite! A delicate gentle design which suits me admirably. There is something Celtic in it, and organic — surely you have added touches of your own to the design on the gun? I'm lost in admiration for your skill. The amethyst is a brilliant addition. Thank you so much, I shall treasure it.

This is far too grand for a birthday present, but I will accept with good grace. Perhaps you will consider making Mildred something too. She is going through a difficult time and may need cheering up. You can now put your tools to peaceful use!

I don't suppose the police have apologised. I am inclined to believe it was police incompetence in your case, rather than malicious distortion of the truth, as in mine. Either way they do not come out well in my book. But you are in the clear and that is what matters. I would advise you to leave the matter there. I have no time at all for people who spend quantities of their own and the public's money on greedy libel cases. It is not dignified.

Now, would you like to visit me for a few days? I feel you need a break. Life has been particularly tense for you and the sudden release may be something of an anti-climax.

My house is large, as you may remember. You can be as private as you wish. Perhaps you could time your visit to include October 7th? Sally is making her debut on the stage. Has she told you? Her topic may interest you but I will keep it a surprise.

I hope Sally has thanked you properly for the cheque. She is a dear girl but inclined to be off hand where letter- writing is concerned. I am trying to get together a block booking for her performance and would be happy to save a seat for you. Here is another chance for you to be a good outgoing uncle, Adam!

If you decide to come, would you bring your bread recipe? Bread-making is a skill I've never mastered and I'm keen to learn.

I am so glad everything has turned out well.

Affectionately,
Grace

Monday 5th September

Dear Mildred,

A brief note in haste. This morning I noticed an estate agent walking around your property. By the time I had crossed the park he was gone. Surely you don't intend to sell? Perhaps it would be wise to check with your daughter and son-in-law. It occurs to me they may be taking your future into their own hands. I know you would have informed me if you had come to a decision.

Be strong minded, Mildred. You have many friends here who are missing you. Cio-Cio is putting on weight, I don't know how to control her. She sends you a special miaow.

Affectionately,
Grace

P.S. A sign has just gone up! Harcourts. Phone 476-8752.

DRAGON'S TOOTH

Driving down the hill to the Community Centre, Grace feels the familiar ache. She is lopsided, the car out of balance; her friend's absence strikes too deeply at the normal order of things. Sherry after bowls is a lovely, distant memory.

'Mildred, Mildred,' she says out loud, shaking her head in frustration. A fifteen-year institution should not be broken without serious discussion. Grace needs, urgently, to talk with Mildred. She is convinced the wrong decision has been made; that Mildred lacks older friends in Christchurch with whom to weigh pros and cons; that family pressure has been too strong for her.

Grace is not surprised to find that news of Mildred's move has reached the bowls club.

'I see the auction sign is up,' says Cynthia Peddie, straightening her back to ease a cramp.

'Oh good bowl!' roars old Mrs Peddie. In fact Grace's bowl is well short — still within Mrs Peddie's limited visual range.

Grace and Cynthia exchange a smile. Overflowing her chair, walking frame parked beside her, the old lady is, it seems, immortal.

'I saw that smile!' she shouts. 'I'm not gaga, you know. Anyone can see the bowl is short, but poor Emily needs encouragement, if she's to improve.'

'Grace,' says Grace.

'Exactly, dear. Pace! Pace, Emily, and we'll make a bowler of you yet!'

'You'll miss Mildred,' says Cynthia, and touches Grace gently on the arm.

Over afternoon tea, Les Comfrey develops the subject of the auction.

'She'll regret it, mark my words. Line the pockets of the auctioneer, that's all. Money down the drain.'

'You don't think it's saleable?' asks Grace. This is a new thought.

'At auction? No chance. What do you say, Jack?'

'Well, Les, I'd say you're right. Not auction material. A pretty little house, mind you.' He smiles at Grace, careful not to offend. 'I could be interested myself if the figure was right.'

'Market's still dead as a corpse around here, eh Jack?' Buying and selling houses is man's talk as far as Les is concerned. Grace can listen in if she likes. 'A hundred and fifty thou — perhaps sixty, at a pinch. What do you reckon, Jack? What day's the auction, Grace?'

Grace is offended. To her, Mildred's house is not a piece of real estate. For nearly fifty years its living room, its friendly porch, its tidy garden have been host to too many conversations, too much shared laughter. She is not ready to accept its sale to a stranger.

'Surely,' she says, appealing to them all, 'surely Mildred is making a mistake? She should keep her independence?'

As usual, Les Comfrey is the first with an opinion.

'Independence is for the robust,' he pronounces. 'I know my psychology, Grace, and I'd say Mildred lacks the backbone for independence. But take me, now. Do you see me moving to the Wairarapa? You do not.'

They are all kind enough to respect Les's pride. In fact they know how disappointed he is not to be invited to live with his daughter and son-in law. Living alone does not come naturally to him. When Les lost his wife, some years ago, he worked his way steadily round the single women in the bowls club, starting with Cynthia. The approach was always the same: a bunch of flowers from the garden, followed by an invitation to dinner at Les's — Chinese takeaways. After dinner came the proposal that Cynthia, or Grace, or Mildred needed a man to do the heavy work, and that he, Les, was prepared to give up his independence to help a woman in need.

'No,' Les continues, 'poor Mildred needs the comfort of her family.'

Grace is outraged on Mildred's behalf, and says so. Shirley Chan extols the virtues of several generations under one roof. Cynthia upholds the case for independence, but is interrupted by her mother-in-law, who has finally caught the drift.

'No Cynthia, you should be more independent,' shouts old Mrs Peddie. 'How many times have I told you? It's time to strike out on your own! Make a life for yourself!'

The ninety-three-year-old, forgetting, perhaps, that she lives in Cynthia's house, not her own, glares at the others. 'Independence is a priceless jewel. At my age I expect a little privacy, but no! Cynthia clings on in the nest. Is this healthy?' She shakes her head, vigorously, wrinkled old face alight with indignation. 'No!' she cries, 'no!'

Old Mrs Peddie's pronouncements tend to close down a topic.

Grace is the only person here with no family at all. For her, living with a younger generation can never be an option. She would like to revive the discussion, but feels exposed. Perhaps self-interest drives her concern for Mildred? And yet the uneasy fear that Mildred will simply fade again, without the familiar structure of life and friends here, persists. She sighs.

'You haven't mentioned Adam for a while, Grace,' says Cynthia. 'Did I hear he was in some sort of trouble?'

Grace smiles. 'He was. But Mildred sorted it out. She knew someone and had a word.'

'Who doesn't she know.' Shirley Chan has always admired Mildred's connections. 'I miss her. You could always rely on Mildred to have the latest news on everything.'

'I saved her life, you know,' shouts old Mrs Peddie. 'The least Mildred could do is stick around till I snuff it. Tell her I miss her, Grace. That should do the trick!'

'At least you've got the Friedmanns, Grace,' says Les. Everyone looks at him. Even taking Les into account, this is insensitive. 'Well, from what I hear,' says Les, defensive now, 'Grace is quite a cosy member of the family. Eh, Grace?'

'Not exactly, Les,' says Grace quietly. There's no use getting bothered about Les. 'Martin and Sheila are upset with me, as you probably know. But I see Sally. She's doing very well, now, at Drama School.' There is pride in her voice.

'No future in that,' says Les. Jack and Shirley Chan agree.

'Sally is imaginative and talented, Les,' says Grace. 'Making money isn't everyone's aim in life.'

Les Comfrey snorts. 'Grace, Grace, I know what I'm saying. Who is happy without money? You're comfortably off. Aren't we all?' He looks around in triumph. 'Indeed we are. Indeed. I say acting is an unwise choice these days. I rest my case.' Grace who knows that Les relies on vigour rather than reason to make a point, decides not to rise to the bait. 'You do talk nonsense, Les,' she says mildly. 'Sally will make her mark.'

'Would she be up to *Shortland Street* do you think? That pays well.'

Grace has something more intellectual in mind for Sally

than soap opera — Shakespeare, Ibsen — but holds her peace.

'Why not make up your own mind?' she says. 'I'm getting up a block booking for her debut.'

This is an exciting idea. Cars and dates are agreed. Grace writes details in her notebook, smiling at her friends. Talk of the Friedmanns has restored her good humour. Adam and Sally, even Sheila, with their various needs, are taking root in Grace's life. To champion Sally's cause, to feel involved in her future, is a rare pleasure.

'Max Friedmann,' says old Mrs Peddie, to no one in particular, 'is a dragon's tooth.'

The rest of the group assume that the old lady is wandering, but Grace is startled. The Greek legend is apt. For every dragon's tooth that Jason planted, up sprang an army. Max's death has brought forth an army of Friedmanns.

'Where did you learn mythology?' she asks old Mrs Peddie.

'Don't expect me to follow that modern nonsense!' the old lady booms back. 'I'll stay put in my own home! They can carry me over the doorstep feet first in a coffin!'

This, fittingly, brings afternoon tea to a close.

'Cynthia,' says Grace, 'why don't you bring your mother-in-law round for a glass of sherry?'

9th September

Dear Grace,
We are having a lovely run of weather here in Christchurch, I hope it is the same with you and that my new camellia is making a good show. I thought when I put it in that you would enjoy it from across the park.

Well dear, I've been slow to write which is not like me, but I have had a difficult decision as you realise. Thank you for all your advice and for the messages from the bowls club.

I think in the end it is best if I settle here with my daughter. You won't approve, I know, Grace. I'm not clever like you to marshal arguments and I will miss the house and garden, but it seems to be meant. The family here are very insistent. They suggest it is selfish to live in a large home designed for family use. I hadn't thought of it like that really, perhaps they're right. Well, they have built a dear little granny flat in the back yard. It would be ungrateful to turn it down, Grace. It's too small and too close to the house to be let to a stranger.

Judith, my daughter, you've met her I think, the thin one, feels that Wellington is too far away if something goes wrong. She has a point. It was hard for the family last year, when I was so ill and they had to drop their jobs and run to my bedside. They're so good to me, I feel I owe it to them to make things easy.

Well, Grace, I can hear you disagreeing but the die is cast. My son-in-law has put the house on the market, it has been empty too long, he says. A non-productive unit, he calls it.

I would be grateful if you could pop across to the house before the auction to check that all is clean and tidy. The real-estate people won't notice little things. No doubt several of the neighbours, not to mention the bowls club, will want to pry and I wouldn't like them saying I had let things go. Do write a good account of the auction itself if you can bear to go. We can only hope someone suitable buys it, I don't like to think about it, Grace, someone else making changes.

Never fear, I'll come up from time to time. I know you will make me welcome and we can have a good laugh again over a sherry. Sherry is not the same without you, Grace, I have to admit!

Affectionately,
Mildred

Monday, 12th September

Dear Mildred,
What a difficult time you are having! My heart goes out to you. It's true, Mildred, that my head is full of reasons why you shouldn't make this move. But it is also clear to me that you have made your decision, and cannot bear to go though any more arguments. I will miss you more than I can say, but there it is.

You are right about the auction: everyone is planning to go! Les and Jack have their own views about the reserve price, and even old Mrs Peddie will be there. She thinks a picnic on your lawn would be a nice idea, though I don't know what the auctioneer will say to that! Yes of course I'll be there and will sound out the new owners as suitable parents for Cio-Cio. Just don't ask me to take her in. I would do many things for you, Mildred, as you know, but not that. She has developed a deep dislike of me, I can tell, though I feed her absolutely according to your instructions.

I hope you are keeping in contact with Adam Friedmann. You are right about the stick of limp celery — a good description! But he is kind, don't you think? And very lonely. I'm trying to persuade him to come to Wellington for his niece's stage debut. Have a word with him. He would appreciate a friendly approach. You're so good at bringing people out, Mildred. I wish I had learnt more from you.

Well, I'll write after the auction; you shall have all the spicy details. Do you remember when we went to the auction of Marge's house and the man insisted you had made a bid! Take heart, my dear. Life will soon settle down again.

With love,
Grace

14th September

Dear Sheila and Martin,
Forgive this letter. I have respected your wishes for some time but fear that Sally has still not written to you. Please understand that I do not condone her behaviour and hope she soon becomes more communicative. Young people these days, I am afraid, tend to take family obligations lightly.

Sally seems well, now, and settled into flatting. Her three flatmates are normal students and care for each other, which is comforting. Sally visits me from time to time and seems reasonably healthy, though I am sure she pays little attention to a balanced diet.

I am fully aware that you do not approve of theatre. Your religious beliefs must, of course, be respected. But I wonder if you would consider coming to Wellington to see Sally perform her monologue? In a sense this is not so much theatre as a series of discourses on subjects related to this country's social history. One could see it as an interesting educational exercise. Several other students will present monologues on different topics. Sally's will, I expect, be excellent; she shows great talent.

I know Sally would value your presence. You are welcome to stay overnight at my home if this makes the trip easier.

Yours faithfully,
Grace Brockie

18th September

Dear Grace,
Thank you for your efforts. I could perhaps have stretched a point but Martin feels we should not go against Church teaching. No doubt he is right. I have written to Sally wishing her all the best.

Yours faithfully,
Sheila

P.S. Are Sally's flatmates all girls, do you know?

22nd September

Dear Martin,
Forgive me if I speak bluntly. Please reconsider your attitude to Sally's performance.

First, the Drama School is a registered tertiary institution, not a theatre. The performance will take place at the school. Surely your church encourages and supports educational effort?

Second, your daughter, Martin, needs your approval. She may not show it outwardly but there is no doubt she misses you both. If I can see her vulnerability, surely you, who have brought her up, can recognise it too. You loved Max, I know, Martin, and were good to him. Sally has a good dose of Max's spirit in her. Can you not enjoy her differences, even if you do not approve of her lifestyle?

You will, I realise, consider this letter impertinent. Sally is your daughter, not mine. Well then, you may blame Max for my openness. Your father taught me habits I do not wish to lose. It is difficult for me to expose my feeling for Sally, for fear of your scorn or pity. I do so for Sally's sake.

Sally is stubborn like you, but you are the older and wiser. You can afford to bend. Please do so.

Yours faithfully,
Grace Brockie

Sunday 25th September

Dear Mildred,
Well, what a surprise! You must be feeling very put out. Les said the reserve was too high, but Jack insists the price was right and that it is simply not the time to sell.

In the end I was not able to attend the auction, but Cynthia came round straight after with the news. She said your drawing room was quite full. Mostly the neighbourhood, of course, and the bowls club. She said it was really strange with all your things still there. Like a party. Cynthia expected you to come out from the kitchen with a plate of sausage rolls any minute.

Well, there were three people she didn't know, though Les recognised one of them and reckoned he would be just a spectator too. Evidently the auctioneer gave a spiel about the history of the place, how you and Perce had built it when there were only farms here, and how well you had maintained the old-style charm. You would have been proud, Cynthia said. Old Mrs Peddie chipped in with extra historical details; the auctioneer would be no match for her, I imagine!

Les Comfrey, trust him, couldn't keep his mouth shut, and gave a knowledgeable little lecture about your fireplace and its unique design, and how his brother had built it. Well, that set one of the strangers off. She contradicted the auctioneer about the house being unchanged. She had visited often when she was a child and distinctly remembered a stained glass window to the right of the fireplace. Cynthia finally made the connection — one of Ethel Eglinton's daughters, who's come back to live in Pembroke Road. You'll remember her of course, Mildred. Well, there was quite a reunion, I gather, with the auctioneer pushed right into the background.

Finally he started off the bidding and there was a deathly silence. He dropped the price, down and down till everyone was embarrassed. Cynthia says they were all looking at the one stranger left, but he never said a word! Les insists he was a real-estate stooge, there to push the price up. He could well be right for once. Then in the middle of all this silence, old Mrs Peddie turned and rammed her stick into the wall. 'Dry rot!' she cried, 'Look at that! Dry rot!' as if she'd encountered the plague. The woman doesn't know her own strength, Mildred. Cynthia says not to worry, she'll see the hole is mended. Les, of course, the expert, darted forward and diagnosed dry rot indeed. Mrs Peddie can be most surprising. Les says not to worry, it's only a patch and his son will see to it for you.

Well, my dear, it turns out there were no buyers there at all. Perhaps it would be better to wait? Though your family will advise you, I'm sure.

I am a little worried about Cio-Cio. Cynthia has been putting out food, but she hasn't been seen for some days. She is a strong-willed cat; I suppose she will return in her own good time.

Sally Friedmann, Max's granddaughter, called today to see how I am getting on. You would love her; so much energy and fun. Would you believe she is doing a small performance at the Drama School based on my Springbok Tour arrest. Your rescue will get a mention too. I wish you could come and see it. On second thoughts we might start arguing the issue all over again! Is Adam planning to come? Sally's parents don't believe in theatre. How can people call all this dourness Christianity? I have been quite sharp with them. I'm not at all sure I'll be able to be there myself, now, and Sally desperately needs approval. Persuade Adam if you can. His niece is very talented.

You are right, your camellia is a picture; I am enjoying it.

With love,
Grace

27th September

Dear Grace,
Oh dear, you poor soul, lying there on my path with no one to help! Adam has just told me the news, he had it from Sally. Grace, you will play the stoic. Surely you could have told me. Now I want all the details, you know how I like a good hospital story. But a break! That is nasty at our age, Grace, you need proper care or you will never hear the last of it.

Adam says Cio-Cio tripped you up, she will get a good talking to. I expect she has disappeared from shame, the bad girl.

Well Grace, this has tipped the balance. Judith can say what she likes but I'm needed in Wellington. Clearly this is not a good time to sell. I have suggested Judith puts Simon in my granny flat and charges him rent. That way they won't miss out. If a son stays at home he should contribute I say, though whether Simon who is six foot four and his enormous dog will fit in my wee rooms is questionable!

Well that is for them to sort out. I am coming up straight away, and will be over with some of my pea and ham soup before you know it. Let's hope the gardener has left some parsley in the garden.

I don't believe for one minute that there is dry rot in my living room. Please tell Les to wait till I come. I never heard such nonsense. Perce insisted on heart rimu. In any case I have my own builder as Les very well knows. I did laugh over the auction though. And cry, to tell the truth. The thought of all my friends there in my house. I tell you what. We will have a party when I return and you are up and about. And this time I *will* appear from the kitchen with sausage rolls.

Of course I remember Ethel, who wouldn't. Fancy that obnoxious daughter of hers standing still long enough to notice my stained glass window. She is quite right though — it let in water and Perce had it removed before I could get a word in. The child must be 65 now if she's a day. I must look her up, no doubt she has mellowed.

Well Grace, my dear, you were right all along, I belong in my own home. It is like a weight lifting, it should not need a friend with a broken leg to make me see sense.

Adam says he's coming up for Sally's performance. You had better book me a seat too, though I'm surprised you are prepared to let the whole world know you have a criminal record. Adam says he will arrange a wheelchair and get you there by hook or by crook. He seems very fond of you in his own serious way. I hope you are not getting carried away again, Grace!

Well, I must fly. There's packing to be done!

Say what you like, I believe that cunning Cio-Cio has planned the whole thing!

Affectionately,
Mildred

THEATRE PARTY

'Oh dear, what a fuss,' says Grace, but her eyes are alight with excitement. Each arm round the neck of a burly drama student, enthroned like a queen on their laced hands, she is carried in style up the steep stairs to the Drama School. Her plastered leg, jutting forward, nudges Mildred.

'Now now, you boys,' says Mildred, pausing to puff, 'we're not all in our twenties remember.'

Indeed we are not, thinks Grace, looking at the procession ahead. A last-minute hitch — the loss of the key to the service lift — had threatened, briefly, to derail the theatre party. There was a nasty moment when her friends, grouped on the pavement around the wheelchair, Les and Cynthia propping up old Mrs Peddie, suggested the evening might have to be aborted.

'Oh no!' cried Grace, dismayed that all her planning could be so easily thwarted.

'Wait here,' said Adam, and bounded up the stairs.

'Show-off,' said Les, shifting uncomfortably under Mrs Peddie's weight.

But then a bunch of cheerful students came to the rescue.

'No probs, ladies. They teach us to do lifts, and carry dead weights. It'll be a doddle for us.'

Though the two bringing Mrs Peddie up are making heavy weather of it, Grace notices.

'Whoops!' cries the old lady. 'Steady as she goes, lads. Make way in front!' Her enjoyment of the whole process does not help. Grace holds her breath as the trio threatens to topple. Cynthia steadies from below, Les shouts instructions and the procession moves upwards again.

Their arrival into the theatre causes quite a stir.

'Block booking of eight,' says Grace with pride. 'We've come to see Sally Friedmann.'

'Hey, Sally's told us all about you,' says the bright-eyed lass issuing tickets. 'You're Grace, aren't you? The protester? Hey guys!' she calls to her friends, 'here's Grace! Here's the famous block booking! Get Sally!' The group is surrounded by welcoming students. A second wheelchair is found for Mrs Peddie, plastic cups of wine are offered, everyone wants to talk to Sally's supporters. As the noise level rises, several elderly hands hover around ears; hearing aids are being adjusted.

'Cheers!' Mildred, magnificent in green silk, touches her plastic cup to Grace's. 'Do you think I've overdressed, perhaps?' she adds, looking round at the startling collection of op-shop finery adorning the younger audience members.

Grace smooths her best blue wool over the plaster. 'You look wonderful, Mildred. This is an occasion, after all.'

'It is,' says Mildred. 'I'm home again.'

Earlier in the day, the friends have shared the expense of a house visit by Dawn, the hairdresser. Up to date now on the neighbourhood gossip, and immaculately coiffured, they are ready to enjoy whatever this evening may bring.

Old Mrs Peddie is surrounded by respectful students. The old lady's hands are dancing. A snatch of song floats over.

Grace frowns. 'I do hope Cynthia can control her mother. She was in music hall evidently.'

'What hasn't that woman been in, Grace.'

'Well, we don't want her upstaging events. This is Sally's evening.'

Sally, alight with tension, runs out from behind black curtains and hugs Grace. She notices Adam and her jaw drops. He pats her shoulder awkwardly.

'Uncle Adam! Did you come up specially?'

Before Adam can answer, Sally's attention is riveted elsewhere. Grace turns to look. There in the doorway, looking hesitant and awkward, are Martin and Sheila. The plain formality of their dress, Sheila's kerchief, stand out. They are from another planet. The noise, the coloured lights, the great cavernous barn of a theatre, seem to have stunned them. Grace, who is as surprised as Sally at their appearance, fears they are about to turn tail.

'Greet them, Sally,' she whispers. 'Quick. This is hard for them.'

Sally goes forward as if treading on glass. Sheila gives her daughter a quick little hug. Martin shakes her hand. There is a pause. Grace wills movement. Through the crowd she watches as Sally guides her parents to the desk. There is some discussion. Perhaps they didn't book, thinks Grace. Perhaps they don't know anything about booking. This may be Sheila's first experience of a theatre. She marvels again at Sally's strength in overcoming such a background. And what is it, in this religion, she wonders, that can have turned Max's son away from the world of performance and invention?

Mildred has found a school acquaintance. Grace, marooned in the wheelchair, is free to watch the progress of Sally and her parents. Sally introduces them to the school director. This is a test. The flamboyant woman wears an outrageous orange gown. Her earrings — large bunches of something tropical — sway wildly. It is her glasses, though, that are particularly alarming. The director's eyes are framed by two bright red, luscious lips, a hint of sharp white teeth poised above her eyelids, ready to snap.

This will confirm all Martin and Sheila's fear about theatre, thinks Grace. But the director, charming and warm, is talking animatedly. Sally begins to relax. The director introduces the trio to a respectable couple nearby. There is an awkward pause, then recognition, handshakes, explanations.

Grace lets out a sigh of relief. The Friedmanns will stay now, she is sure. Sally bounces back to Grace.

'Grace! You engineered all this, didn't you?'

'Oh well, just a word . . . '

'A word? It must have taken a Bible full of words to bring them.' Sally laughs. 'And guess what! They've just been introduced to an elder of the Wellington congregation! His son is a second-year. Both sets of parents are justifying their presence like mad.' Sally mimics a serious middle-aged discussion. '"This is a school, after all, not a theatre, sir." — "True, Martin, true. You have to interpret Christian doctrine according to the times." What hypocrites!'

'Now Sally . . . '

'Yes, yes, I'll be good. It's great to see them. And you! You look wonderful!' Sally's eyes are full of love.

'Good luck, my dear,' says Grace.

'Hey, never say that to an actor! It's break a leg!' Sally pats Grace's plaster. 'But you've done that for me. I should be okay.' The tension is back in her voice, though.

In the theatre, the audience watch Dick Seddon haranguing the masses, Te Puea planting potatoes at Turangawaewae, Minnie Dean waiting to be hanged for child murder. After Gladys Moncrieff, queen of musical comedy in the twenties, old Mrs Peddie rises from her wheelchair to congratulate the actor personally.

'You had her just right, dear,' she booms. 'I was in the Diggers, you know,' she explains to a delighted audience. 'Just the chorus, of course. But I knew how to show a bit of ankle. I'll give you a few tips, dear, after the show.'

For a moment the solid, half-blind old lady is transformed. She inclines her head with surprising grace, floats an arm out to right and left, blows kisses. Then centre of gravity is lost. Les Comfrey and Cynthia dash out to prevent a crash, and the old pro is returned to the audience amid roars of approval.

Sally performs last. In the darkness Mildred reaches across with a quick pat. Grace's fingers are tightly laced. This boisterous, good-natured audience is not quite what she had imagined. She feels exposed. No one will find her life entertaining. Sally has made a mistake. Grace glances behind. Sheila gives her a tight little smile. Sally's parents are on edge, too, Grace realises, doubting, perhaps, their daughter's ability to handle such a crowd.

The darkness is broken by a single spotlight. Sally, in Grace's raincoat, is sitting, alone and silent, on an upturned box. Her feet are primly together, hands neat in her lap. The audience quietens. Slowly Sally looks up. Her eyes are fierce, direct. Grace hears Mildred gasp in recognition; then she is lost to anything but the small, brightly lit person on stage who is arguing a cause. The stage-Grace stands alone, intimidated, on a windy airport runway; she holds firmly to the truth before a belligerent crown prosecutor; there is a passionate plea for personal freedom. Grace and Mildred giggle like schoolgirls as Sally splits and becomes two women enjoying medicinal brandy in a cold car.

Anguish at the loss of a daughter is hinted at, and the loneliness of old age. But the overriding impression is of an indomitable will; of a small, proper woman whose sense of dignity sometimes gets in the way of passion; of an independent spirit, determined at all costs to live a valuable life.

Grace forgets she is watching herself. The performance is overwhelming. The audience smiles with Sally, laughs out loud, murmurs in agreement and, as the light fades, is finally moved to tears. The raincoated old woman holds the crowd for a moment longer, then it is suddenly Sally again and the audience is its own boisterous self.

Amid cheers and whistles, Sally wheels Grace on stage.

'No, no,' says Grace, 'it's your performance not my deeds they're cheering.'

'You're wrong there,' says Sally. 'It's both. Come on, smile like a pro.' And, holding Grace's hand, she raises it in acknowledgement.

Later, there is another round of applause, in another place, as Mildred emerges from her own kitchen bearing sausage rolls. The hardier members of Grace's theatre party are rounding off the evening with supper at Mildred's. The director of the Drama School, earrings swaying and flashing, had invited them all to the after-show party, but was clearly relieved when they declined. So was Sally, arm in arm with Felix, and high on success.

'There'll be loud music and dancing, Grace. You won't hear a thing.'

'I can't hear a thing already, Sally. Congratulations, my dear. You made me feel proud — of myself and of you! You have a great talent.'

'Do you think Mum and Dad thought so too?'

'Oh yes. They must have recognised it. Everyone did. Just don't expect too much. It was a big step for them to come at all.'

'Yes.'

'Build on this, Sally. They've reached out.'

'Yes.'

Grace had sighed with frustration at Martin and Sheila's cool congratulations; at Sally's hurt, sharp response; at the way the couple had slipped away, before the director could speak to them. But it was a start, perhaps. In the meantime Grace will be needed.

Mildred's living-room is buzzing. Adam, pleased to be useful, hands round coffee. Mildred moves from person to person like royalty, receiving welcomes, bestowing sausage rolls. She is in her element, chatting, reminiscing, making sure Grace is comfortable.

Yes, thinks Grace, I was right to push for her return.

'Well,' says Les Comfrey, 'our little lass was the best, no doubt about that. I know a star when I see one, Grace.'

'Rubbish, Les,' booms old Mrs Peddie. 'Grace has her points, but who can compete with our Gladys. Did I tell you about the time when I trod on Miss Moncrieff's train, and it tore right off?' Mrs Peddie is in high spirits tonight, too.

As the story unfolds Grace is holding a silent conversation with Max. 'Well, Max, my dear, I may not be able to unlock hearts like your granddaughter, but I have made progress, don't you think?'

'Not bad,' says the ghost of Max, 'for a crusty old recluse, not bad at all.'

'Crusty recluse? Just because I value solitude . . . '

'Grace, Grace. No backsliding, now . . . '

'No chance of that, the way your family has invaded my life.'

'Are you complaining?'

'I am not, and you know it!'

'I'm counting on you, Grace.'

'All very well. Where are you when a bit of work is needed?'

'Ah well . . .'

'Max, my dear. Thank you so much.'

At that moment a cry from Mildred brings the party to heel.

'Cio-Cio's back! Cio-Cio, you wretched puss! Where have you been?' There is nothing but love in Mildred's voice.

Cio-Cio, fat and unrepentant, stalks into the room. Grace, immobilised, glares as the golden cat approaches, draws down to spring and lands heavily on her unwilling lap.

Grace and Cio-Cio eye each other. In that silence just before decisions are made to leave, the room is filled with purring.

Monday, 13th October 1994

Dear Grace,
As it was my suggestion, the bowls club have delegated to me the task of writing a little note of formal congratulations. I know my formalities, Grace, and this is a moment for well-deserved recognition.

It is not often that the life of one of our members is immortalised on the stage. Your life, Grace, may have been insignificant in the eyes of many, but even the humblest of us have made our contribution to the greater good.

I well remember the time our local Chamber of Commerce took up my suggestion to instigate a special monthly rubbish collection for unwanted household items. The battles I fought to persuade my colleagues! Month after month I planned, presented case-studies, worked on rosters. The Les Comfrey Collection it was fondly known as, then. People have forgotten, these days, from whence came the inspiration. So be it. I need not tell you what a transformation that small suggestion has made in the lives of our community!

But enough of my exploits. Your niece has seen fit to dramatise your simple but worthy life. And a fine presentation it was! The bowls club join me in offering our heartiest congratulation.

Yours sincerely,
Les Comfrey

P.S. If Sally decides to tour the show, I would be happy

to assist you with royalties negotiations. I know my contracts.

13th October

Dear Grace,
I am quite sure that Les Comfrey will write you a load of pompous nonsense, but he insisted he was the one to write.

In fact it was our idea — Mother's and mine — to put on record our thanks and admiration.

The evening out was splendid! Mother hasn't stopped talking about it, and for once she is right. Your niece is marvellously talented, but it was you — your life — which shone. It has opened my eyes, Grace, and I thought I knew you well. What a skill a good actor has, to make us understand so much!

We are all full of admiration for you both. Thank you for organising the theatre party.

We all hope you will be back at bowls soon. Mother says would you like a lesson on the walking frame! She will add a postscript to this note. I hope you can read it.

With love,
Cynthia Peddie

P.S. Grace, dear, this is Mrs Peddie Senior, in person, pen in hand. I told everyone at bowls we must write a note to you.

That was real theatre and I should know! Bravo! Strong content, spirited delivery. I am proud to see stars of the Music Hall era given their proper due. Gladys would have been in tears, I'm sure. Your niece shows talent too, but of course she did not display her dancing prowess. Perhaps she is in need of private tuition? Send her to me.

I have joined the Friends of the Drama School and will offer them my services as a tutor. The time is ripe for a comeback!

Do not laugh. I am perfectly aware my dancing days are over. The days of Variety Theatre are not! Mark my words. My expertise is needed before it goes down with me. Who knows how much longer I can hold on? Do use your influence, my dear.

I would like to be informed if you are planning another protest march. It is important we all do our bit.

On with the fight!

Yours sincerely,
Evangeline Peddie (Mrs)

13th October

Dear Grace,
Les offered to write, but as senior man in the bowls club, I feel it is my proper duty.

Thank you so much for organising the theatre party. Shirley and I enjoyed the evening. It was a first for us, and we would like to be included again. I would be happy to assist with planning a future event.

It must be so hard to allow one's private life in public like that. Especially such a shameful occurrence as conviction in law. We are impressed with your foolhardy courage.

Our Chinese culture is so different and we must make allowances, I know, but we cannot help to feel uneasy that you have persuaded Mildred to return. To us her family's loss is great.

Never mind! To each his views. No doubt this will be subject for discussion again at bowls! My wife has learnt your way of argument and the subjects you raise become much-repeated weekly topics. It keeps us young and surprises our children!

All the best with your leg. You are a strong woman.

With kind regards,
Jack and Shirley Chan

13th October

Dear Grace,
Martin and I are sorry we did not have a chance to speak to you after the performance. We were anxious to get on the road.

The evening was painful in so many ways. However suffering is not new to us, and we do not regret attending.

That Sally should choose to dramatise the life of a stranger, when there are many shining examples within her family and Church circles is hard to understand, or bear. Martin says we must accept it; that she is going through a period of rejecting the values we taught her to respect.

I am afraid that this is more than a phase. Artistic freedom, the wayward self, inherited from their grandfather, Max, has been too strong. My children are lost.

We do recognise that Sally has talent. At least she used clean language. The student portraying that dreadful murderer was quite shameless. It was not easy to remain seated in the face of such evil. Whatever induced the girl to portray such a monster? I simply closed my eyes and prayed for it to end.

We both felt Sally was easily the most talented. We can only trust she will exercise proper judgement in choosing future roles.

It was at least heartening to see her healthy and happy. Thank you for insisting we make the effort. Would you let us know of future performances by

Sally? Perhaps you could furnish an outline of the story and the character she inhabits, so that we can make our own decision about suitability.

Yours in Christ,
Sheila Friedmann

POSTSCRIPT

On the footpath, next to the park, two women are standing. Silhouetted against the morning sun, they could be mother and child, but both are, in fact, in their eighties. One, in plaid skirt and teal jumper, makes more of a statement as she stands; is more solidly rooted to the ground. Her hand is raised in regal acknowledgement. The other, tiny and birdlike, leaning on crutches, simply smiles. Their attention is on a shuttle taxi as it pulls away. The tinted glass hides whoever is inside: one or a crowd. Perky, blue and white like Grace's border, the taxi rounds the corner, brings its bouncing trailer into line and is gone.

'A nice enough lad,' says Mildred. It is more of a question.

'Nice enough,' agrees Grace. And after a pause: 'He would like to have stayed longer.'

The larger woman smiles and picks up a gardening fork.

'It seems a pity to break up these polys,' she says. 'Are you sure, Grace? They will still flower for a month.'

'One or two won't be missed, Mildred, they're so vigorous. The white will look good against your fence. Goodness knows your frontage needs urgent repair, you're back in the nick of time. But wait a bit,' Grace adds, 'we'll have a cup of coffee first. You can inspect my new kettle. Adam has given me one that turns itself off.' She laughs, remembering something.

Later, in Grace's sunny porch, Mildred expands on her subject.

'I do think you are wise to keep Adam at a distance, Grace. The younger generation are all very well in their place, but a little goes a long way, don't you think? Judith is still on at me to shift to Christchurch, but I've made up my mind. Their lives are too rackety for me. I like a bit of space around the day.'

'Yes,' says Grace.

'And Cio-Cio doesn't like change.'

Mildred shifts a little stool and gently levers Grace's damaged leg onto it. She pats the plaster as if acknowledging a friend.

Grace smiles. Today the crinkles round her eyes curve upwards; there's energy in her voice.

'Well Mildred, you're right, of course, but I hardly think the wishes of a cat should sway you.'

This is an old argument which both women pursue with pleasure.

'Adam,' says Grace, returning later to the subject in hand, 'would like to bury himself here and look after two old ladies. That may solve some of his problems. Even some of ours. But it would create others.'

'Well for one thing, Grace, how long will we last?'

'And for another, Mildred, to be honest I find him a little heavy-going. Of course I wouldn't say so.'

'Of course not.'

'He's welcome to visit now and then. And we'll keep up the letters.'

'I take my hat off to you, Grace. I feared you were going overboard again.'

Mildred sips her coffee. She looks into the distance. Her illness shows now only as a shadow under eyes that are steady and warm.

'Have you noticed,' she says, 'how few of that generation can hold their end up in a good conversation? Judith is the same. They simply dry up before you've got into the swing. I put it down to the fifties. A drab decade. The grandchildren, now, they grew up in the seventies; it softened them. I don't care what you say, Grace, they'll be able to keep a good chat going. When they've a few more years under their belts, of course.'

Grace is doubtful. 'But will they have the background, Mildred? The depth? I can't hold out much hope.'

The argument moves back and forth. Points are scored, decades examined, agreement finally, comfortably, reached.

Out in the sun again, Grace and Mildred bend over the garden, ready now, in their own good time, to divide the polyanthus.